THREE INCIDENTS AT FOSTER MANOR

P.T. PHRONK

Three Incidents at Foster Manor

Copyright © 2019 by P.T. Phronk

Cover and interior illustration and design © 2019 P.T. Phronk, with some elements from Book Cover Zone and Vellum.

First edition (1.2)

Published by Forest City Pulp

@ForestCityPulp

http://www.forestcitypulp.com

PART I
A MYSTERY

CHAPTER 1

My arrival at Foster Manor was not without emotion.

Since losing my family, I'd thrown myself into work, which involved long hours at the dreary office followed by crashing at the apartment. Neither location had any sense of history, nor did they invoke any passion. The only time I felt anything at all was when my mind, without any conscious intention to do so, conjured up its own dark emotions. Being forced on this field trip, driving far from my apartment in the city, gave my mind far too much time to wander. To conjure.

My wandering thoughts could kill me if I let them. I knew that. It's why I normally welcomed the long hours of work that kept my mind occupied.

I twitched when the storm behind me lit up trees surrounding the road with a blinding flash of lightning.

The previously invisible trees exposed all their autumn colours, conjured from the darkness.

Gary had called me earlier that day, though it felt like yesterday. *Amy! Are you free?* And I was—of course I was—so I listened to what he had to say, throwing myself into work once again to get my meandering mind back on course. Some millionaire client used our services when he renovated his old home, three hours north of the city. He'd screwed it all up, as our clients do, and he needed someone to go up there and unscrew it. Because he was a millionaire—*maybe even a billionaire,* Gary added, practically drooling—a regular tech wouldn't do. This needed the *white glove treatment,* as he called it, but have you ever tried typing with gloves? You're bound to make a lot of mistakes.

If it doesn't take long, you could be home by ten? Gary phrased it like a question, hoping for an invite to my apartment as an answer. Gary was another thing I threw myself into after losing my family. He was a living distraction.

Okay, maybe Gary was distracting me for a short while before I lost my family too—I should be more honest with myself than I was with Wes. I was running away from my family even before they were taken from me.

I wouldn't be home by ten. A few wrong turns and a malfunctioning GPS system had delayed me from getting on the right highway, and it was already getting dark.

Lightning flashed again, and I thought I saw a white truck among the trees, way off the road. Perhaps there were other roads back there, winding through the dense woods to come at this mansion from other angles. I'd grown up in a big city, where roads were generally straight enough that you didn't change direction unless you wanted to. Up here, the roads twisted and turned, transforming from concrete to dirt, heading downhill, then uphill, still winding, tires slipping on gravel, the next twist threatening to toss you right into a lake.

When I turned again, the truck was gone. Maybe I'd passed it. Maybe it was a trick of the lightning. Maybe it drove into a lake.

The storm came together unnaturally fast. Dots of red clouds on the horizon heralded its arrival, then suddenly filled the sky like ink in water. These storms had been getting more severe every time—this already looked to be worse than last night's drizzle, and the environmental catastrophe had ensured that even a few drops of the burgundy rain could make a person sick. I'd be safe in the car if worst came to worst, but pulling over in the middle of the woods in the middle of the night wouldn't be the most wholesome camping trip. Especially not with that white truck out there. Something was unsettling about seeing another vehicle so far from civilization, out in this forest, where only animals and reclusive billionaires belong.

A sigh of relief escaped my lips; I wouldn't have to

sleep in the car tonight. As the road's path put fewer trees between me and the house, it gradually came into focus. I'd studied Foster Manor's blueprints before, but never seen it in person, so driving up to it now was like meeting a friend from the internet. The home was new entwined with old. Its core was an ancient farm house, but it was now connected to an equally old carriage house by a newer wing. Another modern wing was built later, trying to match the character of the original buildings, but the yellow bricks were too clean compared to the blackened patina of the house's ancient bones.

My company's addition to the house was newest of all, but that wasn't visible from the outside. The only clue was a sign stuck in the flower garden: *This house protected by APT Security.*

Thunder cracked overhead. I parked in front of the garage, then leaned forward and tilted my driving glasses up to check the sky. None of that awful rain was falling yet, but it would start soon. The clouds swooped and swirled, like they were reaching down to tap on the home's slate roof, or topple one of its many chimneys. The windows below held only blackness—the house could have been abandoned, except for the dull glow showing through textured windows on the first floor.

A security camera hung from the awning over the front door. It didn't belong with the rest of the profess-edly aged home, standing out like googly eyes stuck on a Renaissance painting.

I made sure my pony tail was all professionally bundled up, then hurried to the front stoop. I pressed the doorbell between the intricately-carved wooden doors and the wide windows that gave me a view of an expansive foyer.

A tall man with greying hair opened one of the doors. "Welcome! Oh, looks like another storm. You'd better come in." He stepped aside to let me in. "Amy, correct? Sorry, Ms. Burnett?"

My married name. I'd been meaning to get that changed. "Just Amy's great. Pleasure to meet you in person, Mr. Foster."

He took my coat and hung it on a rack by the door. "Craig is great too. You know, for my name. I'm not— I'm not saying I'm great." As soon as his hands were free, they began to fidget with each other. "I appreciate you coming at such short notice."

"Hey, it's what we do," I said, hoping I didn't come across as sarcastic. Because that would be *so* out of character for me.

"Yes, but with the unexpected storm and every-thing, you know. It's appreciated, by me, by all of us." I heard murmuring voices as Craig led me across the marble floor, past the carved banisters of the double-wide staircase leading to the second floor, and down a hallway lined with art. The frames were filled with a haphazard mix of subject matter—from photos of a pair of children to a sickly-thin woman to paintings of dragons that would have been more at home in a kid's room. Lightning flashed outside, and through a pair of glass French doors to my left, I spotted a dining room that had been set up for a meal but not used. The white linens took on a red tinge for a moment in the odd light of the storm. A moment later, thunder crashed, momentarily silencing the voices down the hall.

"So, do you live with family?" I asked, careful not to be specific about a wife, or a husband, or kids, as I'd discovered how awkward and painful bringing that up could be as soon as I lost all of mine.

"My son, yes, and well … yes, my daughter as well. My daughter lives here." He coughed into a clenched fist. His hair was full and well-trimmed, sticking out in the front like a little cliff over his forehead, but its grey sheen gave away that he was much older than me. He was in good shape, with a deeply-lined but handsome face and a thin build that made his arms look a little too long for his body. I only noticed how old he really was when he coughed, his eyes squinting to accentuate the crevices radiating from them and the bags underneath them. "How about I introduce you to my son and the others, then show you to the control room?"

"Sounds grand," I said.

The hallway opened into a modern kitchen on the right, and to the left, a family room with a mishmash of old and new furniture, gathered around a wood-burning fireplace that must have emptied up into one of the many chimneys I had spotted from the outside. The people sitting around the fire were as varied as the furniture itself. They stopped talking when Craig and I walked into the room.

"Everyone, this is Amy Burnett, from the security company. She's come to troubleshoot the, um, the issues with our system."

"About time," muttered a pale man with a goatee sitting on a couch near the far wall.

The others ignored him. A short and burly black man near the fire rose from his chair and approached me with his hand outstretched.

"This is—" Craig began.

"I'm Marcus," the man said, shaking my hand with a firm grip and a smile that instantly eased my increasingly frayed nerves.

"Marcus is a long-time friend of the family, and the greatest cook in the county."

"There isn't much competition around here, Craig," Marcus said.

"The point remains, the point remains," Craig said quickly, as if they'd done this little bit many times before. "And that's Ash back there. He takes care of the facilities, including the security systems."

Ash looked up from his watch and made eye contact with me for a split second, which I suppose he considered a greeting. I usually didn't judge people too quickly, but—ah, I'd almost forgotten that I'd promised to be more honest with myself. I always judged people quickly, and I immediately judged Ash to be a prick.

Neither Marcus nor Ash were wearing anything that

gave away their roles. I guess I expected a white chef's uniform and a jumpsuit, respectively. "You both live here? That must be a nice perk of the job, huh?"

"I also get to eat the best food in the county," Marcus said, and winked. While everyone else laughed, Ash muttered something; I only caught "never leave work, never stop working."

The third person in the room cleared his throat. There was a moment of silent anticipation while we waited for him to say something, just long enough to be awkward. "I live here too."

"Yes yes, this is Caleb, my son," Craig said.

Caleb Foster couldn't have been older than seventeen, but the bags under his eyes matched his father's. His hand vibrated slightly as he half-stood from his chair to shake my hand.

I scanned the dark corners of the room, where knick-knacks on tables and shelves cast oddly-moving shadows in the flicker of the fireplace. "Your daughter lives here too, you said? It must be nice to have your family so close, especially with everything going on outside, and being so far from the city."

Caleb's head snapped down so he could get a better view of the floor. Marcus turned to Ash, who subtly shook his head.

Craig cleared his throat. "Ah, yes, well, we'd better get down to business then."

Craig stepped aside and gestured for me to follow him. "Ash, come with us, will you? You know this stuff better than me."

Ash pursed his lips and stood. A sudden clap of thunder filled the room, making Caleb jump and nearly fall out of his chair. "I'll come and see too. I want to see," he said.

"Well, I sure as heck am not staying here alone," Marcus said.

We returned to the kitchen, then turned toward the foyer where I'd entered the house. I fell behind as I gawked at the small touches that made the house unique. Intricately-carved crown molding lined the ceiling. Every wall was adorned with ornate wooden panels. Looking through the cluttered rooms, I could see that many of the windows—even those in the modern portions of the house—were topped with old stained-glass illustrations. When the lightning flashed, it lit up a glass cow in the living room's window.

"We get notes!" Caleb said, his sweat-dappled face suddenly an inch from mine.

"Excuse me?"

He made sure that his father and Marcus were occupied talking to each other, then pulled a piece of paper from his pocket. "Threats," he said. "You're the security company, right? Dad ignores it, but maybe there's something you can do."

I scanned the note, which was typed on paper creased from being folded and unfolded too many times. I caught the gist of it: *abandon this place ... you have the money to go elsewhere ... we know about the safe room ... we will return.*

I thought about that odd white truck in the woods. "Have you told the police?" I asked.

"They're useless. Wouldn't get here in time even if a psycho with a chainsaw scheduled a visit in Dad's calendar."

Christ. What had I walked into here? "So this is why your father built the ..."

"The control room is upstairs," Craig said, climbing the ancient wooden staircase that was the centrepiece of the foyer.

Caleb gave me a worried look with his watery eyes, then rushed to help his father up the stairs. Craig's legs shook with the effort of climbing each step. I followed, but paused at the landing halfway up. The windows there gave me a view of the back yard, which had so much concrete and furniture that it could've been considered a third wing of the house, and the newest one, by the looks of it. A swimming pool, glowing from lights embedded in its walls, took up most of a court-yard. At the far end, a half-indoor / half-outdoor shelter was done up like a tiki bar.

"It's beautiful, wow," I said.

"You'll have to refilter the pool after the storm," Craig said to Ash.

"Right," Ash said. He'd fallen behind and was checking his phone.

Marcus stared out the window and bit his lip, his eyes on the horizon, where pinpricks of headlights on a highway were barely visible across a vast canopy of trees.

I stared at the view a moment longer, and the others indulged me. The rain started then. It looked normal at first, but as the droplets hit the water below, I could see a slight pink mist in the glow of the pool lights. Most storms looked like this since the environmental catastrophe.

Lightning flashed in the distance.

Thump thump! It was behind us. Then two more thumps. The sound came from below—someone at the door. I twitched and whipped around, my heart thrashing in my chest. Something about the way these people were acting made me jumpy.

"Oh, thank God," Marcus said. He must have seen the shock on my face. "It's okay. That's probably my daughter. She just finished work, and we're supposed to go for a late dinner, but I don't think that's going to happen with all this going on outside." He glanced at the pool, now alive, frothy with the heavy raindrops pouring from the sky. "Anyway, go ahead. I'll get the door."

Craig led us up the second flight of stairs while Marcus headed for the door and I heard it creak open. When I got to the top of the stairs, I peeked over the railing that overlooked the foyer. A girl in her late teens, maybe early twenties, let herself into the house, using the edge of her coat to wipe rain from her face, then checking over her shoulder as if to make sure the door was still closed. Marcus put his arms around her and whispered something in her ear. Her eyebrows creased with worry. She looked down, as if she could see something that I couldn't in the patterns of the marble floors.

I caught up with Craig, pushing past Caleb, who was trying to get my attention again.

"Mr. Foster," I said, "you did call me to fix a malfunctioning security system, correct? Perhaps it's just the storm making me nervous, but I feel like I'm being left out of something here."

He inhaled too quickly, which made him cough again. When he regained his breath, he waved me forward, toward a hallway leading back into a wing of the home's upper floor. "Yes, yes, I'll show you."

"Will you just tell her?" Ash asked.

Craig's lips tightened. "Ash takes care of the security system. He's quite diligent about always arming it at the proper times and keeping the software up to date. So I'm not sure what could possibly have gone wrong to make it all go offline."

We passed more bedrooms. Caleb pointed at the closed door to one of them—this one had a crystal doorknob that was so old it was turning yellow. "I don't go in that room. Ever," he said, a lopsided smile on his face as he stared at me with glassy eyes. I wasn't sure what he wanted me to do with that information.

"Okay, um, cool," I said.

Further up the hall and to our right, I spotted a second kitchen, though this one was bathed in darkness except for when lightning flashed yet again. I could hear the rain beating at the windows and the roof above us. The storm was getting worse, making my chances of getting home tonight between slim and jack shit.

"Wait, it's *completely offline?*" Caleb's voice was squeaky. "I thought it was just the safe room."

He bickered with his father, who tried to assure him that he didn't want to incite worry by telling his son that the security system was, in his words, completely buggered. Caleb looked like he was going to cry when he found out he'd been lied to, and rubbed at the pocket in his jeans that he'd pulled the note from.

Ash grabbed my arm and turned me toward him while the others got further down the hall. "You shouldn't have come," he said. "I mean, he shouldn't have called you. These people have money, but sometimes they don't have a clue. You know the type. Maybe you should just go. This is something we could've solved over the phone if he just let me handle it."

His hand still gripped my arm, harder than I liked. "I don't think I'll be going until the storm is over," I said as I pulled away from him.

"Yeah, alright," he said. He ran the hand that had grabbed me through his wavy brown hair. The man looked boyish, with a face that was rounder at the bottom than the top, like a teardrop, yet simultaneously gave off an older vibe, perhaps because of the anachronistic goatee and an olive corduroy blazer that would have been at home in the '70s. "No skin off my nose. Just realize that you're walking into a shitshow here. And I *do* keep everything up to date. I wasn't even here when it all screwed up—everyone's been on vacation, so I finally had some time off. So don't be pinning all this on me just because I have the passwords, alright? I'm not the only one who does."

Was that his angle? Was he trying to get me out of here to avoid the blame for this screw-up?

"Ash? The key?" Craig asked, now frazzled by the argument with his son, a strand of grey falling free from the ridge of hair above his forehead.

"Look, I'm not here to pin this on anyone," I said to Ash as he pulled a keychain from his pocket. "I'm just here to fix the problem, whatever the hell it is, and you can bet your ass I don't want to be coming back here on another stormy night, so I'll tell the owner of the system—that's Craig—exactly what went wrong and how to make sure this doesn't happen again."

Ash scowled, then opened his mouth to say something else, but Craig gestured for him to hurry. He stuck a key into a door near the end of the hallway, just before another stairway.

We entered an office. Sometimes clients would insist on the control room being a tiny closet with a wall of equipment and monitors, like you'd see in movies, usually with a security guard snoozing in front of it. Craig had been more sensible, and had us set up our hardware and software to connect to a regular computer monitor in a regular office. Probably not *his* office, though; I had only known Craig for a short time, but I had a feeling the men's magazines and old comic books lying around were more Ash's deal.

Craig turned on a light and they gathered around the screen. For a moment I thought we were looking at a desktop image—an aspirational .jpg of an unattainable luxury car. Then I realized the system was live. The main window displayed the camera's-eye view from inside the perpetually well-lit garage, pointed right at Craig's Lamborghini.

Smaller windows along the top of the screen showed the other cameras installed throughout the house. One pointed away from the front door, and had most certainly watched me as I'd first gawked at the house. Another showed the back courtyard and tiki bar.

The view of the front grounds panned back and forth to take it all in. I leaned forward. In the drizzling rain, three strange faces hovered in the forest past the driveway.

"Do you see ..." I began, pointing at the display, but by the time the camera panned back to the same spot, it was only forest. Perhaps, like that white truck, I'd read too much into the twisting trees and shrubs. With my nerves frayed, I was prone to seeing things that weren't there—maybe I picked that up from my husband. Former husband. *Late* husband.

Caleb sighed with relief as he squeezed behind the desk and looked at the screen.

"It's fine," Craig said. "It's designed to sustain life for three months."

The thunder crashed outside, and the room's lights flickered.

Craig wiggled the mouse, then tapped the keyboard, but nothing changed on the screen. It still only showed the car in the big window, with a line of tiny windows along the top. "See, Amy? We're locked out. Can't switch cameras, can't do anything at all. And the safe room, well, it's all tied to this, so she's locked in."

"She?" I asked. They obviously hadn't seen anything unusual outside. They were talking about something else. I followed Craig's gaze to the end of the row of tiny windows. The final camera showed the safe room: a bombproof, chemicalproof, soundproof, and all-round impenetrable shelter that could only be unlocked with proper clearance. At least, it did all that when the system was working, which it clearly wasn't.

There was movement on the grainy screen. As I watched, the blur of pixels coalesced into waving arms, pacing legs, a pair of dark eyes set in a fearful face. A girl was locked inside the safe room.

CHAPTER 2

She paced back and forth in front of the yellow door. The tiny window on the computer screen didn't have enough resolution to properly display her face, rendering it as a pale blob with darker blobs for eyes, but the girl could only have been one person: the one everyone had avoided talking about. She was Craig's daughter.

"How ... how did she get in there?" I asked.

"She had access," Ash said.

"Trista would never go in there on her own," Caleb said. "She hated that stupid room."

Craig sighed through his teeth. "Caleb, don't. Not now. You realize how important the safe room is, in case of the remote possibility that ... you know, something could happen. It won't, but it could. We talked about this."

Caleb looked at his father with tears in his eyes. He

19

itched at the pocket where he'd stuffed the note he showed me. "I know, Dad, yeah, I know. But … look at her."

Trista approached the door and pounded on it. I could tell from the way her head jerked forward and the way she clenched her fists that she was shouting, but I couldn't hear anything coming from the basement below, where the room had trapped her. Even if the rain hadn't been pounding the roof and making a racket, the walls of the room, designed to absorb the shockwave of a nuclear bomb, would keep her cries from escaping. At least the room was serving its purpose: Trista was, physically, safe.

"We were all away for the week," Craig said. "Caleb and I took a few extra days off after Thanksgiving to spend with family, while Trista … well, she was doing her own thing. With the house empty, Marcus and Ash only checked in occasionally. Trista must have come home earlier than she'd planned to, then, via some unknown method, got herself locked in there. She's been in there all day. Maybe longer."

"Okay," I said. "I can fix this." I reached for the mouse, and felt Ash tense as I took over the control console that he must have been accustomed to dominating. I clicked on the window where Trista was trapped, to get a closer look, and to activate the intercom so we could communicate with her. I didn't even get to that step. The system prompted me to log in. "You've been logged out. Can you type in your password?"

Ash didn't move. "Do you honestly think I didn't try that already?"

I wheeled around. Ash met my gaze. He had blank eyes that seemed to look past me—a look I'd frequently gotten from dudes, working in this business. Like I was simultaneously getting in their way, yet not worthy of acknowledging. "Just humour the person who designed the system, will you?"

He blinked slowly, then reached over to type something so quickly that it looked like he was randomly pawing at the keyboard. *Incorrect username or password.*

"Try again, slower, *just* in case you mistyped it," I said, trying to keep the sarcasm out of my voice, not quite doing it.

This time he deliberately paused between each keystroke, drawing out the moment while Caleb drummed his fingertips on the desk. *Incorrect username or password.*

"Are you—"

"I'm sure it's right," Ash said. His face had reddened.

"Okay, you're doing great. Craig, can you try?" I asked.

"It's right," Ash said again, but Craig pushed past him and tried his password. *Incorrect username or password.* Ash continued to go on in a detached drawl. "I tried everything already. I tried the forgot password link. I tried resetting the computer. I tried the passcode on the door. I tried—"

"Yeah yeah, you tried everything, yet here we are, at the last step, which is calling the emergency number to get an expert on site. And who is that expert? Oh yeah, it's *me*. Look, I don't mean to be rude, but can you all let me do my job? Go downstairs, have a drink, and Trista will join you in a few minutes."

They bickered for a while longer before Craig convinced them all to leave the room. "I trust this company. They've been doing this since the beginning," he said, then herded Caleb and Ash away.

I waited until I heard their footsteps on the creaky stairs. I got myself a few moments of blissful silence before the wind whistling at the windows and near-constant thunder started getting to me as much as the Fosters. I went through my usual troubleshooting steps, getting as far as I could without going into the diagnostics menu, which would require another passcode.

What was that passcode? I'd set it myself, but it had been so long since a system screwed up so badly that I needed it. This wasn't my job; techs who did this emergency troubleshooting every day would surely have the passcode sitting right at the top of their minds, but usually I was the one who *sent* the techs. All I could remember was I'd chosen a code with so much meaning that I could never forget it. Except that had been years ago, and what had meaning to my past self didn't seem to be particularly memorable to my present self. Whenever I tried to remember, my past became a puzzle made of clear, painful memories, complete except for the one missing piece where the passcode should have been.

I'd have to call Gary and use his code. Damn. Why did my memory have to betray me at the worst possible times?

I took out my phone, but it had zero bars. The storm must have been messing with the signal, or worse, lightning could have completely fried the nearest and only cell tower.

Something rustled in the hallway. I looked up, but nobody was at the door.

It didn't matter. There were two more things to try. I clicked the button to reset the password, which would send an email to the people with admin access to the system—Craig and Ash. I'd go downstairs, get them to check their email, and if that failed, I'd call Gary from the Fosters' landline.

I closed the password window. The girl was now facing the camera, her black, pixelated eyes staring right at me.

I leaned forward. I could just make out the shine of tears on Trista's cheeks as she stared at the camera, her eyes pleading, her shoulders shaking with sobs. The poor girl must have been so scared. Trapped there, scratching at the door, nobody answering her cries as the flames began to boil her skin.

No, I thought to myself, *you're thinking of Todd again. Trista is fine. There are no flames here; all the company's brochures brag about the precise climate control and disaster suppression systems.*

I hurried out of the room and into the hallway. As my footsteps echoed across the house, I heard the rustling sound again, like a broom sweeping a floor, this time behind me.

I turned around. Nothing. Just the sounds of the home's filtration system working, *whoosh-ah whoosh-ah whoosh-ah*, underneath the sharper rhythm of the rain.

I continued down the hallway, but with every step, that rustling seemed to follow behind me. Just underneath the whoosh of the HVAC was another, subtler pattern.

What if, what if, what if.

It sounded like words. Just my imagination again, surely. I took a few more steps, but each thump of my feet was followed by an answering swish behind me.

What if. WHAT IF.

This was more than a rustle. I could hear the growl of vocal chords, the moist slither of a tongue against teeth, right behind my left ear.

I whipped around for one last look back at the empty hallway, then walked as fast as I could, not stopping until I'd practically stumbled down the stairs and the sound behind me was gone, replaced by the chatter of the others in the family room. My nerves must have been completely shot now, conjuring voices from the typical sounds of an old house.

I stopped to compose myself near the kitchen. The fridge there had a few pictures of the kids when they were young—mostly Trista, sometimes with another young girl, Trista's pale skin cheek-to-cheek against the other girl's darker skin. Sometimes Caleb was in the background, and he had those deep-set, haunted eyes even when he was younger. Above the pictures was a sticky note containing shaky hand-written words:

DONT CRY

DONT CRY

What the hell was that about?

❧

I told myself to get it together, then checked to make sure my hair was still held tight in its ponytail before entering the family room. The family was gathered near the fireplace, their conversation heated. They fell silent as I stood before them.

"Well?" Ash asked immediately.

Marcus stood and blocked my view of Ash, which was, I thought, a kind little thing to do. He waved me toward the girl who'd been sitting on the couch beside him.

"Amy's here to get Trista out," he said to her. "Nothing to worry about. Amy, this is Jasmine."

I recognized her from the photograph on the fridge,

where a slightly younger and slightly happier version of her played with Trista. Jasmine's handshake was firm but had a tremor to it. Mine may have been similarly unsteady after the odd experience upstairs, but I tried to make my voice reassuring. "I'm more worried about the storm right now. Looks like a doozy."

Jasmine cleared her throat. "The wind was bad. Dad and I were supposed to go for dinner, but that probably isn't happening. So? Is Trista okay?"

"She's fine," I said. "There's enough food and water in there to last months."

I meant it as a joke, but Jasmine's mouth dropped in shock.

"Trista and Jasmine have been friends since they were children," Craig said. "Always worrying about each other. These two are like peas in a pod, or peas and carrots, or whatever they say about peas and friendship. I guess they had to be close, during those summers when they were the only kids around for miles."

I noticed Caleb's eyes narrow.

Jasmine finally laughed, but there was still a shake to it. "Yeah, good thing us peas got along. That could've been awkward. Can I go see her?"

Craig said it was fine, and Marcus nodded. Jasmine hurried out of the room and toward the stairs like she'd been waiting for a starting gun. She knew exactly where the control room was. It was kind of sweet that the cook and his daughter were treated like family here, but also kind of concerning that they shared access to the security system. The home got less secure with each additional person who had free run of the place.

I asked Craig and Ash to check their email inboxes. The Wi-Fi was still working, luckily, but they both said they had no new messages from the security system. I got them to check their spam folders. Still nothing. Dammit. Had the tech guys messed with the servers without telling me again?

This was getting desperate. I really didn't want to call Gary, especially this late at night. Any dependence on him made me feel more and more like a pile of guilty garbage. Without a doubt, calling in even that small favour would lead to another night of drinks with him, another night in his bed, another morning of regret.

"Okay," I said. "This is fine. There's another thing we can try before—"

Ash interrupted. "Are you going to ask Caleb what he was doing in the office?"

Caleb looked up from staring at the fire. "What? When?"

"There's no *when*. I've caught you in there more than once, messing with the cameras, and every time, I tell you not to come back. If only your father locked down—"

"Now," Craig said, "Ash, I think you're getting out of line. Again."

"Am I? Do you really think the system fucked *itself* up?"

Craig fidgeted with a rip in the old chair he sat in. He began coughing as Ash paced the room, ending up beside me. Ash leaned over and whispered in my ear, quietly enough that nobody else could hear. "He's not long for this world, you know."

Marcus stood and got between Ash and I again. "Could we all just calm right down?"

Ash puffed his chest out. "Calm down? Trista is locked in a room, the tech support here is useless, and Caleb won't even say what he keeps doing in that room."

Craig stopped coughing. "I don't appreciate what you're accusing my son of here."

"I was just …" Caleb started.

"Oh boo hoo, you were just, *you were just*. You broke it. You screwed everything up. It's nothing new, but you can at least come clean with it for once."

I rubbed my temples. "Everyone!" I shouted. My voice had never been loud, but some tone in it commanded attention when I wanted it to. It had always made Wes and Todd stop in their tracks and listen, and it had the same effect here. "I can solve this in one phone call. I just need to—"

A flash of light from the windows bleached the room white for a moment. There was zero delay before the deafening thunder, then all the lights went out.

The phone lines were fried. Cell service too. Marcus said he thought he saw one bar pop up on his phone for a second, but he couldn't be sure it wasn't his imagination. He went upstairs to check if being higher up would help with cell service, which it wouldn't, but he was probably more interested in checking on Jasmine, who was still up there in the control room.

The security system ran off a high-capacity battery, so Trista had the best room in the house right now, not that she knew it. The security station in the control room still "worked" too, in the sense that it had power, though without a passcode it couldn't do anything other than show us the girl suffering in the safe room.

They probably wouldn't be calling it the "safe room" any more after tonight.

At Ash's urging, Caleb used some of his valuable cell battery to light the way to a supply closet, well-stocked with candles.

"I'm sorry about this," Craig said to me after we'd placed and lit tea lights around the house, then returned to the family room.

It was almost ten now, so my hopes of getting home at a reasonable hour had gone up in flames, so to speak. "I guess I'll be following the lead of your other helpers and staying here overnight." After I said it, I blushed, hoped that calling Ash and Marcus *helpers* wasn't offensive.

Craig didn't seem to notice. "We've got a guest room. Several, actually. I think we have more guest rooms than we've ever had guests." He laughed, then shook off another cough.

Marcus returned from upstairs. "She's going to keep an eye on Trista," he said, then headed to the kitchen to make tea.

I sat for a while, staring at the shadows, thinking about the voice I'd heard come out of nowhere when I was upstairs.

"This place is even creepier in the dark, huh?" Caleb said.

A whistle came from the kitchen. Both Caleb and I jumped. It was only the kettle that Marcus was putting on; the gas stove, at least, still worked. "I'm glad I'm not the only one creeped out here!" I said.

"There are stories here. Creepy stories. A lot of them," Caleb said.

Marcus carried cups of tea into the room, the steam rising off of them like tiny, powerless ghosts. I filled the silence. "Do tell. If we're stuck here all night, we're going to need stories."

Marcus rolled his eyes. Caleb looked at his father for approval, who took a tea from Marcus with one hand while mimicking a blabbing mouth with the other. "You guys and your stories. You're going to give this poor girl a heart attack, but go on, don't leave her hanging."

"For me, it's always been because of all the angles,"

Caleb said. "So many rooms, so many corners, so much carved wood in so many different shapes. Sometimes I imagine things. Sometimes I see things. Usually it's just me."

I raised an eyebrow. "Usually?"

Marcus offered me a tea, but I passed. My stomach had been feeling off since my odd fit of nerves upstairs. "Sometimes people see the dog," Marcus said, passing the tea to Ash instead.

Caleb shivered. "Dad did, once."

Craig stopped poking at his chair. "Yeah. That was a year or two ago, wasn't it? Earlier that day I was telling Caleb about the dog I had here when I was younger. We'd always talked about getting another dog, but with me not home much, then the kids getting older, well. You know. Anyway, later that day, I was fixing a drink in the ball room, and I looked up from behind the bar, and there he was, sitting behind the curtain."

I leaned forward. "Behind the curtain?"

"They're kind of see-through, the curtains there. It seemed so real ... my big, shaggy dog, sitting there and panting. He was at the window, you see, except for some reason he was facing me instead of guarding the front drive, like he used to do all the time. His messy hair puffed up the fabric. Except it wasn't really *my* dog, was it? No, his eyes caught the light just right, and ... those weren't my dog's eyes. They didn't recognize me or greet me. And they glowed, like a cat's eyes at night.

"I was thinking, maybe a coyote got in from outside

and got tangled in the curtain. So I walked slowly, around the chairs, across the ball room. And ... and this is the part that freaked out Trista and Jasmine when I told them ... if I was only seeing things, just mistaking ruffles in the fabric for my dog's face, it would go away as I got closer and saw it from another angle, right?" Worry lines in Craig's face got deeper in the flickering light from the candles. "Except the closer I got, the clearer those shining eyes got, and the more I could see just a few grey hairs among the dog's black coat. Still, he's just sitting there! Not struggling against the curtain, just sitting behind it, facing me. And he blinks. He blinks, he licks his lips, I can even hear his tail thumping against the wall as that clumsy oaf wags it."

"Craig's got a very detailed imagination," Marcus said. "I always say he should write a book now that he's got some downtime."

The shadows flickering around the room took on new meaning. The curly sculpture on a side table cast a wagging tail. The edges of a chair formed an animal's quivering ears.

"Well, yes, it could've been my imagination," Craig said, leaning back. "Anyway, that's when I tripped on the edge of a tablecloth. Nearly wiped right the heck out. I was only distracted for a moment, but when I shook it off and looked up again, it was only curtains over by the window."

"What if it wasn't your imagination?" Caleb asked.

I felt weak. *What if, what if.* I let out a sigh. The candles on the table in front of us thrashed and the steam from the cups of tea swirled.

"Poor girl," Craig said. "Our poor guest. You wouldn't know it with all the bickering, but we have good stories here too. This house has served the family very well for generations."

Caleb nodded enthusiastically.

But the candles were still flickering in a way that set *my* imagination off, reminding me of things I'd imagined a thousand times before no matter how much I tried not to. Todd, trapped in that house, alone after being left by his father, by his mother. The flames licking at the door, tendrils of smoke unfurling into the room.

The smell of the tea was making me sick.

"Is she okay?" Ash asked, looking up from his watch.

"I ... honestly? I'm feeling ..." I couldn't even get the words out. "Would you mind showing me to one of those guest rooms?"

Craig and Marcus fawned over me, offering me everything from more tea to Advil to brandy, but I told them I just needed rest. Craig showed me up to the second floor again. More flickering candles glowed down at the end of the west wing of the house, where Jasmine was keeping watch over Trista. Craig touched my shoulder to direct me the other way, past more closed doors than any house needed to have, and into a bedroom. Marcus arrived a moment later with fresh sheets and pillows.

"Thank you," I said, trying to smile. "One quick call in the morning and everything will be fixed. Don't you worry about Trista."

"You're the one not feeling well. Don't you tell us what to worry about," Marcus said as he lit a candle on a desk.

Craig laughed. "That's right. If you need anything at all, just shout. I imagine we'll be up all night anyway."

I had to admit, it was primordially comforting to have these two dads so worried about my well-being, but I did need to rest, so I told them I'd be fine, and thanked them for the accommodations.

Finally, I was alone. The room had probably been Trista's at some point in the past, judging by the pink wallpaper and the mirror adorned with fake flowers. Now it was a guest room. If I had to guess, as soon as she entered her teens, Trista had moved to the room furthest from her parents, even if it was smaller. I'd have done the same thing when I was a kid, if there were any extra rooms to move to.

She'd taken that concept a little further by getting herself stuck in the safe room though.

I took a deep breath, trying to let the little joke I'd told in my own head ease the tension I felt in every muscle. It worked for a moment. I closed my eyes as soon as my head hit the pillow, but I was not asleep for long.

At first I thought it was the muttering from downstairs, or the near-constant thunder outside, that interrupted my sleep. But even in my half-awake state, I could tell that those sounds had become background noise and faded from my consciousness. Something closer had awoken me.

I sat up and pulled the sheets to my chin, like a child would do, in this child's room, and I listened. Nothing. Just the background noise.

Finally, I allowed my mind to wander again. I went over the possibilities for solving this problem with the security system. The passwords had been changed, which could have been due to one of the users screwing up, or it could have been a problem with our back-end password expiry system. It didn't matter. What was stranger was that the emails to reset the passwords weren't being sent. It *could* have been an outage on our end, but the storm couldn't have been interfering with *all* the servers that handled the emails, which were redundant and distributed throughout the world— unless all the dingbats who believed in the imminent end of the world were right.

But there had to be a solution, and I'd find it sooner or later. That was always the difference between me and Wes. He loved mystery for the sake of mystery, finding questions with no clear answer, and no clear *need* for an answer. He had free-floating curiosity.

Whereas me, I solve problems. Even when I left Wes, under the guise of visiting my sister, it was a specific solution to specific problem: I hypothesized that temporarily depriving him of my problem-solving skills would make him realize how much he needed them. How much he needed me. It would fix our marriage and our family right up.

That solution didn't work. Todd died and Wes went missing. *Great problem-solving, Amy.*

Something was breathing in the dark.

I snapped my attention back to the present. I slowed my own breath, gradually exhaling through my mouth so my nose wouldn't whistle.

It was by the foot of the bed—whatever was breathing. I could hear it. The candle had burned out, and I couldn't see anything in the dark, but it sounded like it was just over the edge of the mattress, where I wouldn't have been able to see it anyway. Right where my feet would have dangled over the edge of the bed if I were asleep. Breathing.

No, not quite breathing—panting. *Heh heh heh.*

It stopped. Surely I was hearing the ventilation system again, some fan lilting to one side, brushing against its housing rhythmically.

But then why did it stop?

Something shifted down there. Then I heard the smacking of lips, a slick tongue against skin, then a return to the panting. *Heh heh heh.*

My heart thumped so loud it drowned out the

sound. I couldn't stay here, and the sheets would not protect me, but somehow the thought of putting my bare feet on the floor with whatever was down there felt even more inconceivable.

Lightning flashed. All the angles and furniture cast shadows, but it was too much to take in during a millisecond of light.

Thunder. Then a high-pitched whine from the foot of the bed.

My God, I could just picture that big shaggy dog. The same one Craig saw in the ball room. The same one the family did not own.

I wrenched the pillow out from under my head and put it in front of me. Slowly, I kicked off the sheets, then leaned forward, picked up the pillow—for at least momentary protection against gnashing teeth—and crawled toward the foot of the bed. I peeked over.

Heh heh heh. It was right there. It was too dark to see anything except shifting shadows, but I could hear it. I could smell it. The air was pungent with breath that could only come from a mouth full of sharp teeth laced with bits of raw meat.

The lightning flashed. I clenched up, raising the pillow, expecting it to look up, notice me, eyes glowing.

But nothing was there. Only the scuffed hardwood floor. Of course nothing was there; what could it have been? A dog? A nonexistent dog from some a bored millionaire's flight of imagination?

I let out a breath I'd been holding for a minute, then

put the pillow behind my head and lay back. When I listened again, I could hear nothing unusual, just the patter of rain, and the muttering voices from downstairs.

The voices stopped. A floor creaked as someone climbed the stairs, probably giving up on the day, heading to bed to try sleeping. A rattling cough let me know it was Craig. Pipes in the walls rattled as someone else used a sink. There were a lot of sounds here. Could one of them explain what I had heard?

Sure, just let yourself believe that, I thought.

I was about to let myself take another deep breath, when a woman's scream filled the house. She paused for only a moment, then screamed again until her lungs were out of air.

❧

It was just past midnight in the Foster mansion, and everybody was awake. The residents of the household arrived from all angles, upstairs and down, converging on the control room where the scream had originated.

I arrived just after Craig, who held a panicking Jasmine in his arms.

"There now. Now, there," he said to her. Nonspecific designations of time and place, just words untethered from any actual times, any actual places. When those words didn't soothe her, Craig tried guessing at the cause of her tears. "Did you fall asleep and have a bad dream? No? Did you see someone outside the window? It wasn't one of those hallucinations of Caleb's, was it?"

Marcus entered, with Caleb just behind him. Marcus pushed past me and took over from Craig, holding his daughter close. Jasmine reached for him without thinking, like a toddler flailing for her bottle. Finally, she caught her breath and pointed at the screen. "It's … her."

Craig leaned forward and studied the screen, especially the upper-right corner displaying his daughter. One of his hands came to his face.

Ash hovered in the doorway to the room. I shuffled further inside to make space for him.

Craig turned to the rest of us and seemed to study our faces, his eyes flicking wildly between them. His fingertips caressed the screen, turned at such an angle that we couldn't quite see it, then his hand returned to his face. He opened his mouth to speak, then closed it again.

"She's dead," Jasmine cried.

CHAPTER 3

*T*he control room felt like it was squeezing in around me.

A whimper escaped from Craig's lips. "My baby. No, no … my baby."

Caleb grabbed the edge of the screen and turned it around so everybody could see. It showed the same camera's-eye view as before, from up high in the corner of the safe room, looking down at Trista. Except this time she wasn't pounding on the door, she wasn't screaming, she wasn't crying. This time, she was lying on the floor face-down.

"She's sleeping. She's sleeping, right? Right?" Caleb asked nobody in particular.

But we could all see the red. We could all see that not a single pixel was moving. No, that wasn't true; as I watched, the pool of blood around Trista's body did get slightly larger.

"I gotta … I gotta call …" Ash muttered, turning to leave the room.

"No!" Craig said, pointing at Ash. "Close the door. Nobody leave this room."

Ash closed the door, as he was commanded to do, and six people crowded around the desk. My elbow nearly knocked over a porcelain Hummel figurine from the book shelf behind me as I squeezed in, my shoulder against Marcus's.

Everybody stared at the screen for a long moment, silent. She still didn't move. The blood stopped spreading, and I spotted more red, in small spots leading from Trista to the yellow door of the safe room.

That's when I saw it—writing. The image was too blurry to read it, but the smeared blood beside Trista had the structure of a short word. Her final word.

Craig began to cry, which caused him to cough. Caleb stood like a statue, even paler than before, trembling. Ash muttered something in his ear. Jasmine continued to sob quietly in her father's arms.

My heart was breaking. I couldn't stop thinking of Todd, my son, but was that selfish? What else could I do? What could I possibly do?

Finally, Craig roughly grabbed the keyboard. "We need to get in. We need to help her," he said, his eyes flicking up to me. He mashed the keyboard until the system prompted him for a password again. He typed it in slowly, hunting and pecking with one finger.

D O N T C R Y. He exhaled, then continued typing. *D O N T C R Y.*

They were the words from the sticky note on the fridge. Which meant everybody in this house had access to the security system using the very insecure password—or more accurately, *former* password, because of course, it still didn't work to unlock control of the system. *Incorrect username or password.* Craig stared at me, his eyes red.

I checked my phone. Still no signal, probably owing to the continued pounding of rain outside. I shook my head. "No internet or phone. I can't get the failsafe passcode without a signal."

A flurry of movement erupted beside me as Caleb elbowed Ash aside and opened the door. "I'll go down there myself. I'll chop that door down if I have to."

"No!" Craig said. "We need to stay together."

He was right, of course. This had become a murder scene, and someone in the room must have become a murderer. The writing beside her, and the splashes of blood leading from Trista to the door, told me that she hadn't done this to herself—someone had killed her and escaped, then she'd written something, like the name of her killer, in her own blood. I found myself trying to examine everybody's hands, looking for the apocryphal red one, but they all moved so fast, and so many thoughts and memories intruded on my reasoning.

Nobody mentioned the writing. Did they not see it? Or did they fear angering the killer?

Despite Craig's warnings, everyone spilled out into the hallway like the room was on fire. Caleb ran down the hall, then down the stairs.

"Are you going to just let him go?" Ash asked Craig.

"What the hell am I supposed to do, Ash?" He collapsed, his back against the wall, his head in his hands.

Ash tightened his lips and shook his head.

"We could leave, find a pay phone, call the police," Marcus said.

Everyone had a different reason for that being a bad idea. Craig said he couldn't leave her. Ash said the nearest place with a landline was an hour away. Through tears, Jasmine said the storm had gotten worse and we'd risk damaging our lungs just getting to the cars. The environmental catastrophe had made homebodies of us all.

I didn't have to say anything, but the need for us to stay together was underlined by the household's immediate reluctance to involve the police. We shouldn't have let Caleb take off.

Jasmine finally stopped sobbing, but she still couldn't stop glancing toward the door to the control room, as if Trista would walk out of it at any moment. Marcus held her at arm's length and brushed her hair away from her eyes. "Honey," he said, "did you see what happened? How did Trista get like that?"

Craig pried his head from his hands to pay attention.

"I ... I went to check on her. I've been checking on her. I stepped out, just for a few minutes, just for half an hour. I came back and she was ... she was like that."

Craig's face lit up. "Like that. What if she's only hurt? Let me check. Maybe we can get in there in time to help her." He stood on wobbly legs and returned to the control room.

Ash watched him go. "Man's delusional. His son just became the heir to the family fortune and he lets the kid wander off right after the first in line bites the dust."

Marcus started toward him. *"Bites the dust?* What the fuck is wrong with you?" Ash puffed up his scrawny chest, and Marcus's fists clenched, but then Jasmine fell into another fit of tears, and her father deflated to go attend to her.

Ash shook his head and turned his back on Marcus, then said quietly, so only I could hear, "Family, man. Wife squirts out a kid and suddenly the smartest dudes become delusional saps."

"Amy!" Craig shouted. "Come in here, now!"

I found myself scowling, which made Ash smirk. He clearly lacked some sort of compassion mechanism in his head, but in that moment, with Craig issuing an order like I was his servant, I kind of felt where he was coming from when he openly resisted this strange family. Perhaps that open hostility became charming with time, which explained why they kept him around.

A metallic clang echoed throughout the house. That must have been Caleb in the basement, trying to chop open the door. We'd designed those safe room doors to withstand everything from blowtorches to ballistics. An axe, or whatever he was using, would only chip the paint.

Where did he get a blade so quickly? Was he the only one with a weapon here? The reality of the situation started to set in: one of these people had killed Trista just minutes ago. That person could still pose a danger to the rest of us.

Marcus glanced from Ash to Craig to me, never taking his eyes away from the rest of us despite attending to Jasmine. He was probably coming to similar conclusions as me. "Craig," he said softly, his deep voice a rumble. Craig was still in the control room, fixated on the screen. "Craig! It's not going to work. Let's get away from here. We need to talk about this. We need to figure out who ..." He glanced at Ash for a moment. "I mean, we need to figure out what to do."

Craig didn't move. His eyes never left the monitor in the control room while we stared in at him from the hall. People weren't so different than machines—sometimes getting them going just required the right keywords. So I tried a few on Craig. "If I examine the door directly, maybe I can get us in there."

He stirred. "Yes. Yes, let's examine the door."

We went down the stairs to the main floor again, each of us jumping at odd sounds, glancing at every dark corner, keeping an eye on each other. On the main floor, most of the candles had gone out, which suited me just fine, but the others lamented the loss of the light. Marcus rooted through a drawer and found a flashlight, which he handed to Jasmine. It seemed to steady her shaking hands.

The stairs to the basement were at the end of the west wing of the house, past the family room and kitchen, past another branching hallway, and past a laundry room bigger than most people's bedrooms. I tried to picture Ash doing the family's laundry, but couldn't quite do it. Could he even fathom his own role? Did he resent smoothing every tie, polishing every loafer?

The stairs were not as creaky as I felt they should be in an old home like this, and the hallway we walked down was only creepy owing to the darkness, lit by Jasmine's swaying flashlight. They seemed to use this area primarily for storage. Through the open doorways of the maze-like basement, I caught glimpses of towering boxes, piles of toys, stacks of old bricks, wood spiked with rusty nails, and what could have been the oozing form of a deflated bouncy castle.

A metallic squeal, like Freddy Krueger's claws on a chalkboard, came from up ahead.

The hallway opened up into a larger room that seemed, from the look and the musty smell of it, to have been carved right into the earth below the house. I recognized the layout, but walls always looked perfectly smooth in architectural drawings. In person, they were irregular, built around boulders that had sat in the ground for thousands of years and sat there still, perhaps providing some load-bearing functionality for the house above. Even the stone floor had cracked and shifted during the century or more it had rested below the house.

The safe room was another story. It sat in the middle of the basement—a room within a room, sleek and modern, with a few decorative touches I'd designed myself. Customizable doors weren't part of the original product plan, until I stood up in a meeting and pointed out that the people in these rooms could be staring at that door for days, or even weeks, so maybe they should have some say in what colour it's painted.

Caleb scraped the paint off with a rusty crowbar.

"Caleb!" Craig said. "What do you think you're doing?"

No answer from Caleb. He continued chiseling at the edge of the door, causing an awful screech that made the center of my chest vibrate.

"What *is* that crazy motherfucker doing?" Marcus

47

asked, squinting to make out Caleb in the beam of Jasmine's flashlight.

"Don't call him crazy. Please." Craig's voice wavered.

"Sorry, Craig. I didn't mean that." Marcus pulled out his phone and approached Caleb, holding it face-out so the screen provided a bit more light. He touched Caleb's shoulder, causing him to jump and back away, putting an end to that horrible screeching. "Man, that isn't going to work. Ask Amy, she's the expert here. Is whacking at the handle going to work?"

In the light of Marcus's phone, I could see that Caleb had scraped the yellow paint away in a circle around the lever-like handle that opened the door if the correct code was entered on the keypad beside it. "If it worked, I'd be out of a job pretty quick."

"See?" Marcus said.

Craig approached the keypad, which was a full alphanumeric layout, still backlit and powered by the backup battery within the room. He started trying his password again. Then another. Another. If I watched carefully, I'd probably know enough of his internet passwords to ruin his life.

"I thought it would loosen the handle enough," Caleb mumbled. He let the crowbar clang to the ground.

Marcus turned his phone around, and it lit up dark splotches on the ground. Maybe blood. Maybe evidence, except we'd stomped all over it now.

"A signal!" Marcus suddenly shouted. He pointed at his phone. "I saw a bar pop up. Just for a second." He dialled 911, then held the phone to his ear, while Jasmine and I approached him and waited to hear if he got through. I became aware that we'd lost track of Ash on the way here. But there were so many shadows, and so few lights, that he could have still been in the room, looming just outside of view.

Marcus didn't get an answer. "I'll send an email. That way, if I get a signal again, even for a second, it'll automatically send. I have a friend who's a cop. You remember her, Caleb? She was at the pool party a few years ago."

"I was a kid then. I kinda remember. She had her gun with her, and that made me scared, but she also had that hat."

"She loves those stupid hats." Marcus said, his voice deep, rumbling. I admired his ability to conjure some normalcy, even with all *this* happening, but I could tell from his strained voice that he was barely keeping it together. His fingernail clacked against the screen as he attempted to send his email. It didn't go through, but he seemed to think that it would try again if his phone ever picked up a signal. The hope of getting outside help seemed to ease all of their minds, if only a small bit.

Except a moment later, Craig was back trying passwords at the keypad, mouthing seemingly random words as he did it, like some half-remembered incantation.

Jasmine glanced nervously from one person to another, then into the shadows behind us, where Ash could have been, or not. Like me, she knew that one of us had killed her friend. I couldn't rule out any of them, and they couldn't rule me out—though their suspicious glances did fall on each other more than they did on me.

Caleb stared at the ceiling of the basement. "Did you hear that?" he mumbled, but nobody answered him.

The thick air suddenly felt colder.

These people needed me. I was the only objective outsider, the only expert, maybe the only real adult at the moment. When a moment of silence fell over the room, then thunder crashed above, they all looked to me. I got to work figuring out how to figure out what was going on here.

PART II
A HAUNTING

We gathered back around the fire. I wouldn't have chosen to be there, but at least nobody was offering me steaming fucking tea, and the rest of them seemed to calm down enough to function when they were back in the family room, though Craig couldn't stop pacing.

I told them that we needed to stay together. I couldn't quite bring myself to say why—*one of you is responsible for killing Trista and ruining this family forever*—but surely most of us were already thinking it.

During a moment of silence, I felt the sense of being stared at. I looked up to see that it was Ash, the reflection of the nearby fire thrashing in his eyes. "So?" he asked.

My role as the only objective one, the only one capable of making a good decision, was solidifying. I'd have to be a leader here. Unfortunately, I wasn't coming up with any brilliant ideas to lead with. "So, we wait until morning, then get help."

Ash nodded and sat back, fading back into the shadows.

"Unacceptable," Craig said, swivelling at the end of his pacing route. "There must be a way into the room sooner. We don't know if this storm will end by morning. The way things are going in the world, we don't know if it will ever end."

That sentiment was expressed often lately. The environmental catastrophe's origins were still unknown —blamed on everything from global warming to visitors from outer space—and that exacerbated the sense that it could get worse at any moment. It could also end at any moment, but that sort of optimism was generally unacceptable to express in polite company.

My subconscious often served me nuggets of hope, though, and it had been working overtime while dealing with this chaos. "There could be one way in," I said, the idea coming to me in real-time as I said it. "You didn't get the password reset emails, but we were able to trigger the attempt to send them. The problem was somewhere between sending the emails and receiving them." I fidgeted with my ponytail as I thought, ideas still flowing. "If we could receive them in a different way, in a different place, then send the right signal back, we could reset it and get access."

"But we don't have internet," Caleb said. "How could we get the emails?"

"We don't *need* access to the internet. The system is still a network that's designed to be self-contained, and with the right ..." I tried to think of a way to explain it in simple terms. "If we can get the right key, we can open the locks, all locally. We know the email address it's trying to send it to. If we set up an email server locally, then we can get the reset email."

"A man-in-the-middle attack on our own network," Jasmine said.

"Right!"

Ash leaned forward again. "Wait, attack? You're saying this system, which Craig paid his *hard earned money* for, can be attacked?"

He was such a dick.

I explained that with the right knowledge—like, say, the knowledge that comes with being the person who helped design the entire system, and the people who were rightfully supposed to have access to it—any system was hackable. "It's not really an *attack*, except ..." I wanted to say *except to the person who killed Trista,* but that could have come across as hostile. Dangerous, even, to express in the current company. So instead I, lamely, non-sequitured into: "except we need some tools. We just need a computer with an Ethernet port. We can even patch it into the safe room's battery for power."

All the family's laptops were the newer kind, without Ethernet ports. Of course. These people had the money to upgrade their tech whenever something new came out—whereas I was still rocking a phone with a headphone jack, for Christ's sake. They all listed the technology they had lying around, until Caleb muttered: "Trista's old laptop."

Apparently it was a Mac, sitting in storage now.

"I'll show you where it is," Craig said, standing.

"No," I said. "I was serious. We need to stay together."

"Not exactly 'we' though," Marcus said. He pointed at me. "She's good. Can we all agree that she's good?"

They all nodded, tacitly understanding that *good* in this context meant that I hadn't just murdered the heiress to the family fortune. So I got directions to the storage room, trying to repeat them back after I realized I wouldn't be able to memorize every left, right, right, left. Craig shook his head after I screwed it up for the second time.

"It's the one I told you about," Caleb interjected.

The room he'd refused to go in before. I had a vague idea of where it was. "I know exactly where it is," I said. "Be right back."

I became lost almost immediately. I took the stairs near the basement entrance to get to the second floor, figuring I was just there, so I could orient myself, but by the time I was upstairs, I realized I was in entirely the wrong wing of the house, and coming from a different angle made orientation hopeless. Then I got distracted peering into rooms, trying to figure out where the various hallways and offshoots led, and lost my bearings entirely.

It's not like the place was a castle, but the sheer number of rooms packed in, each with identical doors, made it difficult to tell which room was which, and that made it difficult to tell which direction was which.

When I was a kid I saw that movie Labyrinth. It frustrated me how Jennifer Connelly was a smart girl, and she did everything right, yet she still got lost in the God damn Labyrinth because of everyone else's God damn meddling and incompetence.

I felt like I needed to cry.

I also felt like I needed to pee.

I found myself in the upper-floor kitchen I'd spotted earlier. A sliding door led to a covered patio, where the rain was coming in sideways and doing a number on a full living room's worth of wicker furniture, which Ash should really have covered up.

These people had three different living rooms, two kitchens, countless bedrooms. Surely they had a nearby place to take a leak.

I began opening doors. Suddenly, I felt like an invader, intruding on territory I was entirely unsuited to be wandering at night. The next door surely wouldn't be a bathroom, but a kinky sex room, or the stash of illegal secrets that got Trista killed, or …

The next door opened into a completely empty

room. These people had so many rooms that they could just leave one empty. But then the *next* one was almost as bad as my anxiety-riddled fantasies: it was a bathroom, but quite obviously the main bathroom. The one where the master of the house probably kept his medicine, or his condoms, or …

I really had to piss.

I quietly closed the door, dropped my slacks, then hovered for a moment over the seat where Craig likely parked his ass for a shit every morning. When I sat, I could swear it was still warm, but surely that was my imagination. My mind projecting my fears onto my buttcheeks.

I closed my eyes as the relief washed over me. Out of me. I exhaled.

When I opened my eyes, the shower curtain in front of me was moving.

The plain fabric swayed for a moment, then lay still. My imagination again? My breath? I thought of Craig's dog, sitting behind the curtain in the ball room. The same dog that sat at the end of my bed.

I held my breath. I could only hear the white noise of the rain.

I darted forward, nearly tripping on the pants around my ankles, and pulled the shower curtain aside.

The dog was not there. Just like he was not at the foot of my bed. It was only Craig's shampoo, conditioner, and body wash—all Old Spice—perched on the sill of a window that would light up the shower in the daylight. It must have been just lovely in there, getting all soapy, watching the shower curtain sway in the natural breezes of an old house with leaky windows. I allowed myself to imagine being in there with Craig, just for a second. A smile snuck onto my face as I finished up, then stood in front of the mirror. Dear Lord, my makeup was a mess, with dark streaks jutting from the corners of my baggy eyes. I must have cried at some point, even though I could not recall when. I borrowed a tissue from a box on the marble countertop to wipe away the stray streaks, then poked the little handle on the garbage can beside the toilet to toss it away.

The can was filled with a rat's nest of dental floss. Layers of it spiraled nearly to the top, with bits of food and spots of blood all mixed within it.

Craig let his toilet paper hang over the front of the roll.

I didn't belong here. I'd never use Old Spice. I always hung my toilet paper behind the roll. And that horrible floss nest felt like coming across some creature's secret lair—a little personal stash it would return to at any moment, beaks and claws and teeth ready to tear the invader apart.

I took one last glance in the mirror, wiped a bead of sweat from my forehead, and—

An eyeball stared at me.

I whirled around. The eye gazed at me from behind the window. It blinked once, long eyelashes flecked with raindrops. It was far too large. Wasn't I on the second floor?

Lightning flashed. The eye backed away, briefly revealing a lumpy nose beside it before fading into darkness. The shower curtain swayed like someone had swished past it.

I stepped backward, my fingers grasping for the doorknob. This was impossible. No person could reach the second-floor window. And had that eye not taken up far too much of the window pane?

As I spilled out into the hall, the word *giant* was on my lips. "A giant," I whispered out loud. "I'm hallucinating a fucking giant."

The thunder crashed outside, and I imagined it as the giant's thumping footsteps, circling the house, crashing through the forest swinging spindly arms, another barrier to ever getting out of here.

The walls felt too close and my heart twitched like it wanted to exit through my esophagus, threatening a panic attack I hadn't had since I was a teenager. *Thump, thump, thump.* I saw faces in the walls' carved wooden panels and moulding. As my vision faded around the edges, I reached out, like I was the one crashing through the forest in the dark. If I could just reach the stairs and will my legs to carry me down, I'd be back with people. Surely whatever was going on up here wouldn't follow me down and show itself in front of others.

My hand rested on a doorknob to steady myself. The

doorknob was very old and made of glass—this was it, the room with the laptop, which Caleb said he never went into.

I took a deep breath.

It's all in your mind, it's all in your mind, it's all in your mind. I focused on the words in said mind like a mantra. If I could calm down and grab that old computer, I could fix this mess and get out of here.

My nose itched as I exhaled. I could hear faint squealing all around me—surely only the wind whistling through cracks in the older parts of the house.

I closed my eyes and put my hand on the doorknob, picturing what the computer looked like to prepare myself to spot it as quickly as possible. Then I hesitated —why did Caleb refuse to go in this room? After all this, perhaps he had a good reason.

All in your mind.

I swung open the door. The giant stood in front of me.

❧

Jack was there too, stepping off the top of the beanstalk before spotting the giant. For a stained glass window, it was quite detailed, though the perspective was off. Jack's face was portrayed as facing either sideways or head-on, depending on which piece of glass I looked at, like an unintentional Picasso. Additional details were painted on the glass, like the fine eyebrows showing the fear on Jack's face, and the giant's long eyelashes.

I stepped into the room. It was only a window. I must have seen it from the outside when I first got to the house. How else would I have hallucinated a giant in the bathroom window? In fact, it all made *more* sense now, didn't it? A giant in the stained glass window, a giant in the bathroom window.

Two other panels surrounded the one illustrating the story of Jack and the Beanstalk. To its left, the story of Sleeping Beauty was represented by the prince, wearing an elaborate hat with a feather in it, hovering over the poor unconscious girl while fairies around her seemed to be locked in an argument. And to its right ...

"You've gotta be shitting me," I muttered out loud. I refused to look at it for long, because that would solidify it, make it more real. The three little pigs, depicted with hollow eyes and sideways noses thanks to that odd misunderstanding of perspective, would soon wish they could ignore it too. The wolf. Big, bad, shaggy, its fur was painted in detail, arcing off the edges of each tiny shard of glass in little swirls of black and grey.

I rummaged through the junk haphazardly arranged in the room, piled on top of unused antique furniture. I knew I was getting close when I came across the electronics, where a line of iPods chronicled every version released since the very first. I suppose those would be considered antiques now too.

When lightning flashed, I spotted the characters from the stained glass windows staring at me from the periphery of my vision. Their painted eyes seemed to follow me around the room, while simultaneously keeping an eye on each other, Picassoing in every direction at once.

There it was—Trista's computer, placed precariously on top of old computer manuals, covered in dust. I confirmed that it had the right Ethernet port on the side, grabbed the power cord beside it, then sprinted from the room.

Part of my mind told me to just keep running, but a stronger part told me to close the door, so that room would not just be *open* to the other parts of the house. *The safer parts of the house,* my mind automatically labeled them.

So I stopped, and reached into the room for the doorknob.

On the next flash of lightning, every eye in the stained glass mosaic stared directly at me.

CHAPTER 5

$\mathcal{C}$raig saw the panic on my face. "Are you all right? You look like you've just gotten off a roller coaster."

"Where have you been for so long?" Caleb asked, before returning to staring out the window.

Marcus and Jasmine were on the couch, engaged in another conversation. She nodded as she listened intently to her father, whose deep voice and gentle touch seemed to be backing her away from the edge of panic. The bond between them gave me a silver of hope, which calmed my racing heart enough for me to speak.

"I have the computer," I said, holding it up. "Are there tools in the basement?" I looked at Ash, but he just stared back at me blankly.

Craig raised his eyebrows at him. "Ash?"

The caretaker sighed. "There are tools in the basement, but some might be missing. Caleb keeps taking the hammers."

Caleb didn't even look up; he'd been at the window the whole time, peeking through a gap in the curtains into the darkness.

"I won't need a hammer. Jasmine, can you handle an Ethernet cable?" The girl looked like distraction would do her good. Her dark skin sparkled from sweat, and her hands twitched like she didn't know where to put them. I'd been that way for weeks after what happened with my family, and she'd *just* come across her best friend's body. Distractions helped me—even though my brand of distractions always left me with fresh new problems.

Ash put his hand up like he was in school. "Is there a reason for this?"

"For what?" Craig asked.

"All this." He looked right at me. "This futile quest to get in the safe room, when we know we can wait until morning and deal with it then. We're running around and fucking with an incompetently-constructed security system when we could be asleep."

Marcus shot to his feet. "Asleep?" He put a hand on Ash's chest. Ash recoiled, knocking over a picture of the family on the fireplace mantle. "Craig lost his daughter and you're talking about having a God damn *nap?*"

Craig stood. "Marcus, it's fine. We're all on edge. This isn't normal. None of this is normal."

Marcus backed down. He wasn't a large man, but he moved with a bold confidence that suggested muscle under his flannel shirt.

"I lost my family a couple of years ago," I blurted out, talking to buy myself time to think. "I would have given anything to have been there. Even if I couldn't have done anything to stop it, just *being* there … it would have put some finality to it. It may not seem like it now, but years from now, when this day haunts you —and it will haunt you—you'll wish you did everything in your power to get some closure. All of you will."

They stared at me. Nobody knew what to say. I'd left out the part about the word Trista had written in her own blood beside her, which provided another obvious reason for entering the room as soon as possible: it would identify her killer. Their faces didn't give away who had spotted the writing and had the same thought, if anyone.

"Let's get that room open then," Craig said, finally.

Ash nodded, biting his lip, defeated.

The family agreed that splitting up into two groups would be okay, as long as everyone was being watched by someone else. I convinced Jasmine and Craig to follow me into the basement. Marcus had shown me that he could overpower Ash if he needed to, and he could probably lift Caleb with one arm. I realized that I had already formed a theory in my mind about who the suspects were in Trista's murder, even if my theory was based purely on personality rather than evidence. Still, I felt safe with Jasmine and Craig, and felt good about Marcus watching over Ash and Caleb.

The deflated bouncy castle in the basement writhed as if something were living under it. I watched it from the hallway for a moment. Perhaps there were rats under there, in a nest lined with soiled dental floss stolen from Craig's bathroom, feeling very lucky to have always lived in a castle. Perhaps the castle was itself alive, its printed skin still twitching from the muscle memory of when Jasmine, Caleb, and Trista bounced around in it after begging Craig and Marcus to drag it from the basement on a sunny spring day. I could just imagine the castle's rubbery towers thrashing back and forth as the children bounced around inside—while from the real mansion towering above, the stained-glass giant, fairies, and wolf watched.

Perhaps the deflated castle was just moving from a draft.

"Amy? Are you okay?" Jasmine lightly touched my shoulder.

"Sorry, I'm fine." I lowered my voice and dropped back while Craig charged ahead. "Jasmine, have you ever seen anything weird around here?"

"Weird?"

"I mean … it's an old mansion. I'm talking about, maybe, well you know how people say places like this are haunted." I spilled it out quickly, perhaps hoping she wouldn't understand what I said. "Sorry, you probably get this all the time."

A pained smile formed on her face. "The first time I came to visit, late at night after Dad was done for the day, I was totally spooked. I didn't even want Mom to take me out of the car. I still remember this feeling I got, when I looked at the place—like it was watching me. I thought I saw people in the windows, watching us. When I looked, there wasn't anybody there, of course not, but I'd spot movement at the next window, but then when I looked there wasn't anybody there either. Then there's a shadow at the next window, and … you can see where this is going. Rinse, repeat."

"Damn."

"Yeah. It was Trista who said it was nothing, that stuff like that happened all the time. She said that it was nice to have someone watching over you, whether it was her dad or her brother or an army of hollow-eyed spirits." She laughed, though her cheeks sparkled with tears. "*Hollow-eyed spirits.* Who says that? She was so fucking positive all the time, you know? No, you don't know, you never met her. I just can't help thinking that she was *too* trusting, and maybe that's what—"

"You guys coming?" Craig asked.

Jasmine opened her mouth like she wanted to finish her idea, then thought better of it and continued ahead.

At the safe room, Craig was already at the keypad again, trying new combinations. Were they random at this point? Was it even possible for a man to produce randomness, or would his fingers always betray him, revealing hidden corners of his psyche?

I sighed. "That's fine, you keep doing that. Jasmine, can you grab those tools? I'll get the computer set up over there, behind the room."

Behind the room. An unusual thing to say, only possible in this extenuating circumstance of having a room within a room. I opened a panel at the back of the cube-like structure, then tapped into the power supply from the battery inside the room and plugged in Trista's old laptop. That was a special feature of the room—in case you needed to go out into the nuclear wasteland where your house used to be and plug in your Christmas decorations. It could be disabled from inside, but thankfully in this case, was not. The computer booted up and bathed me in the blue glow from the desktop wallpaper: Trista and Jasmine, cheek to cheek, a few years younger. My bet on the consistency of the family's lack of good security practices held true again; she hadn't set a password.

Trista's desktop was a mess. As if she hadn't heard of folders, the picture of her and Jasmine was almost completely covered by files, each with a name like *Week 5, September 12 - 19,* and *Christmas 2009.*

I made sure Craig was still occupied, then double-clicked one of the files.

Trista had kept a poorly-organized diary. Skimming through the files, I spotted archetypal teenage tales that could have been my own. Drinking too much, eating too little, wars between school cliques. She wrote in a sort of code, perhaps giving away *some* awareness of the fact that anyone who opened up this computer could read everything. Friends and enemies were referred to by initials. Two regulars, appearing on nearly every page, were referred to only as HE and SHE.

Another weekend in town. SHE brought weed, so we smoked under the bridge again, and talked about the future.

...

HE is always there. I feel him staring even when he's outside.

...

When I bring HIM up, SHE gets uncomfortable. We don't fight about it, because I don't think we ever fight, or could fight, but she pushes harder about getting out of here, and that makes me uncomfortable, but maybe I'm uncomfortable because she's right.

I leaned in close and pretended to type something to hide my snooping as I got closer to more recent entries.

We researched universities together. The way SHE looks at me ... omg, sometimes it scares me so much. I don't even know what to do with myself. I'm crying, what a mess!

...

HE is planning something.

This felt like meeting Trista's ghost.

Yeah, you read that date and time right ... it's 4 in the morning. I've written about the spookiness here before, but ghosts never scared me. HE is something different, the way he haunts the house. Does he not sleep? It's the middle of the night, and I heard the creaking outside my door again, and again my door was open even though I shut it, I'm sure I shut it. The whole hallway smelled like black cherries. It must have been HIM.

"Fixed it yet?" Jasmine appeared beside me. I snapped the laptop shut, which was about the dumbest thing I could do to avoid appearing suspicious. I tried to smooth it over by pretending I needed two hands to lean in with the flashlight and inspect the screws that held the back panel in place, even though I could recite the model number by heart.

"Hopefully this'll do it," I said. I asked her to hand me the correct screwdriver, opened the panel, and together we got to work. Jasmine was good with tools, and even better with computers, so it didn't take long to hijack the room's outgoing communications. It seemed to get her mind off of things, too, and the tremble in her hands disappeared.

Getting my mind off things was more difficult. Jasmine could be SHE. Craig could be HE. The girl who had last been frightened of SHE and HE lay dead just metres away.

"There!" I said, willing confidence into my voice. "Craig?"

"Mmm?" He was still tapping away at the keypad.

"Okay, just keep doing what you're doing. That's great."

Jasmine leaned over to look at him. "Won't he mess it up?"

"That's exactly what we want him to do. After every ten attempts with a wrong passcode, the room will send a warning and an email with a code to reset the password. We catch it on this laptop by intercepting the email to Craig, send the reset code back, choose a new password, and we're in."

Jasmine handed me the end of the Ethernet cable coming out of the room, anticipating the next move before I even said anything. "A Janus attack."

"I haven't heard that term since my training courses. Yeah, also known as a man-in-the-middle attack, like you said earlier. You're good, girl."

Jasmine smiled politely. Her hands were steady as she passed the cable to me. "I like the Roman god name better. The dude with two faces, in charge of beginnings and endings, looking to the past and the future at the same time. I guess that puts us right in the middle."

"Stuck in the middle with you," I sung, horribly out of tune with the old song.

Jasmine smirked and groaned. She got my dumb reference. I was starting to like this girl.

SHE.

We watched Craig, his face glowing in the backlight of the keypad, as he continued trying passwords. It would be just my luck if he finally got the right one just now.

He leaned back every time he tried one, his mouth agape in anticipation, waited a second, then tried another. I counted the attempts. Four, five, six.

Grab a crucifix.

Someone shouted upstairs. The muffled voice was followed by thumping footsteps, accompanied by the creak of the floorboards above.

Craig shook his head like he was coming out of a trance. "Was that Caleb?"

"Oh no, what now?" Jasmine said.

"You two go," I said. "I'll finish this, then we can all go in together and figure out what happened."

Craig gave one last forlorn look at the keypad before Jasmine gripped his elbow and led him upstairs. I was alone, as I preferred to be whenever I was working on something complicated. I took Craig's place at the keypad and tried some more incorrect passwords, much more efficiently than Craig had. *000*, I typed, then hit enter. It flashed red: incorrect.

More shouting came from upstairs, then more stomping. The creaking of the floor seemed to go on a bit too long. It turned into a deep growl, and it wasn't coming from above. I whipped around and aimed the flashlight into the corners of the room, but in this carved-out basement, there were too many corners, too many jagged shadows.

It's nothing, I told myself. *There are no ghosts, just teenage girls thinking up fantasies in an old house. The ghosts are no more real than the bouncy castle in the other room.*

I tried more codes. *111, 222.*

The darkness seemed to close in on my peripheral vision. *Not real, not real, not real*, I chanted to myself, but the bouncy castle was *real* even if it wasn't actually a castle, and the growling sounded like it was right behind me, and my ponytail tickled like it was swaying in a light draft. A lover's breath.

333. Enter.

Refusing to look back, I ducked around the safe room to the computer behind it. I checked my Janus program for the email. Nothing.

Padded footsteps approached from the darkness, but it wasn't real, couldn't be real, so I double checked my hack, tightened every connection. If an email had been sent to the Craig's email address, I'd have intercepted it. I didn't.

It meant someone had messed with the settings.

Someone had intentionally changed the backup email address before any of this happened. It wasn't a mistake, or a messy coverup of a mistake—it was premeditated sabotage in service of a careful plan. Someone had meant for Trista to be in that room, and for us to be unable to get to her.

A chill caused my whole body to clench. I inhaled sharply. A smell like rotting meat filled my nostrils.

I raised the flashlight. Canine eyes reflected back, glowing. The shaggy black dog lunged, sending a flurry of yellow teeth at my face.

My body acted on instinct. Luckily, instinct was smart enough to bring the flashlight with me as I turned and bolted. The shadows jumped around me with each step. The basement around the safe room was full of junk that I hadn't seen before; my impression of the place had been all wrong. There was even another door I didn't know about—Door #2, leading who-knows-where.

I circled the room, the sound of claws on stone close behind, then headed back the way I'd come from. It was the only known route to safety. Door #1.

The bobbing shadows had folded back ears and legs coiled back, ready to pounce. The darkness had eyes.

Instinct sent additional motivation to my feet, making them sprint faster. I passed the door to the room with the bouncy castle in it and turned for just a moment to look inside.

Maybe I just tripped. Maybe something clamped on

my foot. I spotted grey, which was maybe the floor, or maybe it was the oozing, writhing bouncy castle reaching out for me. The flashlight left my grip as instinct prepared my hands to cushion the fall, but it happened too quickly. I fell sideways, then backward, and felt the sickening thunk of the back of my head against concrete.

Footsteps approached, and soon the dog would be upon me, tearing at my windpipe. It didn't matter much, because I already couldn't breathe.

The dog's eyes glowed. No—no, those were not eyes; the light was too bright. It was not a dog upon me, but a woman standing over me with another flashlight. My head hurt so badly that my vision blurred. It had to be Jasmine, coming back to get me.

I blinked very slowly. "Jasmine?"

She leaned closer, so I could see her face. It was not Jasmine's face.

I could barely hear; the blow to my head had sent my ears ringing. Yet some part of me understood what she was saying, and that part was able to respond.

"That's your name?" I asked in response to her distant words. I felt pressure at my elbow as she helped me up, and got my stumbling ass to the stairs, where I had to sit down again.

"Yes, Mae Carmichael. Marcus is an old friend. I came in through the cellar door in the basement."

Mae wore a hat like I'd never seen before. The green wool of its brim seemed impossibly stiff, and a knitted yellow flower at the side seemed to grow right out of it. A gun was strapped to her side, barely hidden by the thin, flowery blouse she wore. I could hardly focus on her features, but she had dark skin, and bright, kind eyes.

"My my, what a big hat you have," I said. "I'm sorry. I'm … I'm a friend of the family's too, I suppose. I've been helping with the security system. You're the cop, aren't you? The one Marcus mentioned. You got his email? His call for help?"

"Yes, I am here to help. I didn't expect to find a stranger in the basement passed out on the floor, however."

I thought of Trista. "It's actually much worse than that."

"I know about Trista. Oh, poor Trista, my gosh." Mae's voice became sad as she told me a story about the family, which I wanted to pay attention to, I really did, but the back of my head killed, and when I lifted my ponytail to touch underneath, it felt like the surface of a fuzzy water balloon.

"There was a dog," I said, interrupting her. "A big one, looked more like a wolf. It was right in the other room. It's aggressive."

"Oh, dear, there's no wolf."

"I'm under quite a lot of stress. Perhaps I imagined—"

"No," Mae said. "Sorry to interrupt you, dear, but I think I know what's happening here. It's another haunting. The wolf you saw was a ghost."

My head cleared a bit. Nobody in the family had spoken so directly about the mysterious happenings in this place. "You know about all this?"

"Oh dear, oh darling, it's been like this forever. I don't mean 'forever' literally, of course … though come to think of it, it may be closer to the truth. Maybe I do mean forever."

"Craig said he saw a dog before, in the ball room."

"He told me all about it. Father—their father—he keeps his head in the sand, maybe only to protect the kids. He sees these anomalies, but he won't say anything, or do anything about it. Marcus is less tactful, and at least he has the decency to deny that anything is happening at all. We're very different in that way, which is part of what I love about him. Regardless of what either of them say, this place is sensitive to spirits, like many other places in the world. Like me."

"Like you?"

"I'm a police officer, and a damn good one." She laughed heartily—an odd sound, given the circumstances. "Part of that's because I've always been a bit … attuned, you could say. I've always been in touch with spirits." She hovered around me like she was a nurse, checking me over. With one finger under my chin, I was able to lift my head, though it kept wanting to topple down again.

"What have you seen?" I muttered.

"Too much, dear. When Craig and Marcus weren't around, I used to tell Caleb, Trista, and Jasmine stories all night long. And they'd tell me their own. It led me to research this place, and the nature of spirits."

"What ... what is the nature of spirits?" I asked. It felt like the lamest question in the world, but I couldn't properly put my thoughts into words at the moment.

"It starts with Jack. There's always a Jack, isn't there? In folklore all the way back to England and Ireland, there's always a hero, and he's the one who protects everyone against the giants, the half-man half-monsters, or the wolves. There are always wolves. But when the stories came here to Canada, over in the Atlantic provinces where I'm from, Jack was fighting ghosts instead. New Brunswick was so full of ghosts that they had to transform their imaginary heroes to stand up to different foes." She sighed. "But Jack couldn't help himself; when he came over the Atlantic, he brought some of his companions with him. His wolves, for example. One gets so attached to one's enemies."

I rubbed the sides of my head, willing the pain and the fog to go away, and Mae's story wasn't helping. "It kind of makes sense, but I don't see how it explains what's going on here, in this house."

"The ghosts were already here. They always have been, probably always will be, but they take many forms. The stories, and Jack, they told lessons for our ancestors about how to defeat them. Jack is the hero that takes charge and stands up to whatever shapeshifting evil he needs to stand up to. He takes action when others wouldn't. Do you understand? That's all it takes. This is what I always told the children, and I believe it made them feel better. Not only that, but I hope it made them better people."

I felt like the house was watching me carefully. Like the eye of the giant outside was piercing through the house's many layers to see what my next move would be. "Tell me more," I said. Because fuck it, I could take action if nobody else would. I could be Jack.

So she told me, and I half-listened, about a simple ritual to come together and put forth a vessel to confront the spirits of the dead. It was the first time she'd described spirits as belonging to the dead.

"Wait, what about Trista?" I asked. Mae stared at me from under the brim of her hat, waiting for me to continue. "She's dead. If there's something about this place that is making the dead restless ... and this ritual can bring them forth ... could we contact her spirit? Could she tell us who killed her?"

"I ... I don't know if I spoke correctly. I suppose anything's possible," Mae said, though her voice seemed distant now.

I felt overwhelmed by the possibilities. I couldn't

get in the room to find out who killed Trista and give closure—or perhaps even survival, if the killer wasn't done—to this family. I'd failed at that. But if I were to confront this problem head-on, maybe trying something insane like contacting the spirits of the dead was the only way to bring this family some security, if only for the night.

My head dropped no matter how much I tried to hold it up. I probably had a concussion.

"Dear, you're on the right path. Everything you're doing is putting things exactly how they should be," Mae said, and her soothing words seemed to deepen my trance.

The next thing I knew, I was upstairs, Mae was gone, and the residents of the house were screaming at each other.

CHAPTER 6

*E*veryone fell silent and stared at me. They had gathered in the foyer, around the home's front door. Craig coughed, out of breath from raising his voice. The others' faces were in various stages of anger and frustration, frozen that way when I walked up and interrupted them.

"What if it was her?" Ash said.

"What if *what* was me?"

Jasmine rushed forward and took my arm. "Of course it wasn't Amy. She was in the basement this whole time. Are you okay? You're pale."

"I fell on my way up. I'll live." I shook my head, which was quickly clearing up, the adrenaline starting to reach my brain again. "What is Ash trying to blame on me?"

They each turned toward the front of the house and stepped to the side. Someone had written on one of the windows flanking the front door.

OUR TURN

The first R was backward, like a child had written it. It was written in red. It could only be blood. Another message, like the one Trista had written on the floor in her own blood, except this one was not locked away, inaccessible until morning. Lightning flashed as I approached, backlighting the message, making it glow crimson like it was another stained-glass window.

"It's written on the outside," Jasmine pointed out, squeaking her finger against the glass.

"Or between the panes," Caleb said.

Marcus sighed. "I told you, that's stupid. This isn't a slammed door in the night or a mirage in the dark. Your sister is dead and you still want to blame it all on fairy tales?"

"I'm not stupid," Caleb muttered, then cringed and backed away from Marcus.

Craig inhaled and Marcus braced himself, all of them ready to start bickering again, but I held up a hand and they stayed silent, looking at me for guidance again. Their Jack. "Mae is here. I talked to her about what's going on here, and it's not the first time you've all encountered something unusual, is it? This place is special. What if this writing is Trista, reaching out to us? She tried it before. Maybe I'm the only one who noticed, but she wrote something on the floor of the safe room before she died. In red. I couldn't read it, but this could be her second attempt. Maybe the spirits need a turn to talk."

Ash smirked. "So Trista's a ghost. Why not? It's not the craziest thing you people have come up with tonight."

You people. He was the only one I wasn't already thinking about as part of the family.

"That's an insulting idea," Marcus said.

Jasmine shot him a sharp glance. "Dad, we have to do something."

"We do have to do something," Craig said softly.

"Let's give Trista a chance to speak," I said, thinking about the instructions Mae had given me. The ritual.

"A séance? Let's be clear—is that what we're talking about here?" Marcus asked, but didn't give anyone a chance to answer. "I'm not messing with a damn séance. I'm making a damn casserole for everyone, because all this is making me *damn* hungry."

Jasmine looked like she wanted to say something, but I spoke first. "It's fine. I'm hungry too, Marcus. A meal will do us all good."

This technique always worked with my family, and it was working with this one too. Whenever Wes was into some impossible project or investigating some new mystery, I'd back off, let him do his thing. Same with Todd, as long as he came home safe. I could see my family in this family—and Marcus's adjacent family— each of them so different, together but going in different directions.

Craig cleared his throat. "Where's Mae? You said she was here? She must have gotten your email, Marcus."

"I'm not sure," I said honestly. My memory was a blur since meeting Mae in the basement. She must have led me upstairs, but I couldn't remember actually parting with her. "She said she was going to figure out what happened here, so maybe she's checking the control room. She told me about how to do the ritual."

Ash laughed. "The ritual. Why the fuck not?"

Craig was already heading back to the family room. He nodded, his poof of grey hair bobbing up and down. "Let's do it, then."

"I'm up for a séance, if it can help Trista. I'll try anything," Jasmine said, her voice shaky. Ash shrugged, then told Caleb to grab more candles.

Did I even believe in ghosts? Of course I didn't. Probably. But if gathering around the family room holding hands could get these people through the night, kill a few more hours, maybe bring out more information about who killed Trista, then why not?

And if a ritual could get rid of the feeling that the wolf was still there, licking its lips while it watched me from every shadowy corner, well, that would be nice too.

A fine mist hung in the air, and the house smelled like

onions. The candles had a layer of dust on them from being in storage for too long, so they gave off acrid smoke. Marcus's cooking in the kitchen across the hall also contributed to the appropriately hazy atmosphere for the séance.

We'd pushed the chairs and couch back so we could all sit on the floor in front of the fireplace. Candles surrounded us with more fire. I went through the steps that Mae had outlined, which I could only half remember. The other half I filled in with what I'd seen in movies.

Sweat dripped down the back of my neck as I leaned over to grab the upside-down wine glass from the floor. "This is, uh, a spy glass." That name hadn't come from Mae. It's possible I made that one up entirely. I pointed at the sticky notes we'd put on top of a cutting board— one with *Y* printed on it, and one with *n*. Ash had made it lowercase, probably just to be a dick. "You've seen Ouija boards before. First we'll confirm that a spirit, or spirits, are present. Then we'll start asking questions."

Marcus stared at us from the kitchen. When he caught me looking, he quickly got back to his casserole.

"In the first stage, it is important to test the spirit with counterfactual claims." That line came directly from Mae. "I suppose that means we should see if it can distinguish truth from fiction."

All were silent for a moment. The flames all around me appeared so bright. If this ritual had even a chance of contacting the dead, what if a spirit other than Trista showed up? Could Todd's mirage travel this far, from the burned-down husk of my former home? If he appeared to us, would his skin be pale, as it had been in life, or black, as it was in death?

"I've got it," Jasmine finally said to break the silence. She placed her fingertips on the edge of the wine glass's base. Craig, Caleb, Ash and I did the same. It wobbled a bit on the cutting board, but remained between the two letters. Jasmine closed her eyes, perhaps to hide that she was tearing up. "Trista loved biology class. Is this true?"

The glass remained stationary.

Jasmine grimaced. "Come on Trista. If you're there, we need you."

A slight wobble.

A tear fell from Jasmine's eye. "You can do this, girl."

The glass shot to the left, toward the Y. I didn't exert any extra pressure. It didn't feel like anyone else did either. The beauty of a wine glass is that it would topple before moving if anyone suddenly pushed from one side.

"It's saying yes," Caleb said, smiling. "That's right. She always loved animals."

Jasmine shook her head. "She does love animals, and she thought biology would be about animals, so she took all the classes she needed to major in biology at university. But ..." She laughed shakily. "I think she was thinking of zoology, and besides, she was more of a writer than a scientist. She *hated* grade twelve biology. All cells, no animals."

"So this séance is bullshit," Ash said. "Caleb thought it was a yes, so he rammed on the glass."

"I barely touched it."

Craig cleared his throat of what sounded like a large wad of phlegm, then looked down, addressing not just the Ouija board, but the basement below it. "Trista, honey, who did this to you? Who took you away from me?"

"It's a yes or no board, Dad," Caleb said.

Ash shook his head and looked at me. "You can probably see why Trista's plans to go to university bucked the family trend." He tapped the side of his head. "Brains a bit lacking here."

"Jesus, Ash, really? Now?" Jasmine said.

"She wasn't going to university," Craig said, seemingly oblivious to the insult.

Jasmine opened her eyes, which were suddenly full of fire rather than sorrow. "Well, actually, she was."

"With whose money?"

"She's your oldest child. In a few months, you won't have any use for money. Do you really need me to say it?" Jasmine held his gaze. As if to underline her implication, Craig unsuccessfully suppressed a cough.

My jaw dropped and sweat beaded up on my forehead, but Ash's smug grin implied that he was enjoying this. He pointed at Caleb. "That makes it a lucky day for number two in line," he said, as if it was a casual, offhand comment.

Craig stood up. The floor creaked. He pointed toward the hall. "Get out of my fucking sight, Ash. You too, Jasmine. I can't have this discussion again, not now, not without ..." He choked, cleared his throat again. "Not without her here."

Jasmine stood and muttered apologies to Craig, tears streaming down her face. Just when Craig's face was about to soften, Ash made another biting comment, and it started all over again.

"No no no," I muttered, trying to keep them all together. It was now more important than ever. I'd been holding on to an odd hope that it wasn't one of these people that killed Trista, but some freak Rube Goldberg-esque accident within the safe room. Now, I'd determined the entire security system was purposefully sabotaged, and their continual bickering was starting to reveal longstanding conflict that I could only half understand, making the nebulous family dynamics gradually coalesce into flickering shapes resembling motives. "Let's finish this," I said, but my voice felt small.

"Dad, just sit down," Caleb said.

"Didn't this chick say Mae was the one who came up with this insane idea?" Ash said, pointing at me. "Are we all just going to believe her and pretend that makes any sense? I don't see Mae here."

Craig ignored him. "Do you really want to finish

this, son?" He leaned forward to grip his son's chin between his thumb and forefinger for a moment and examine his face. "Are you going to like the answer?"

The cutting board jumped, tilting to one side and sending the wine glass toppling. A chip of glass came off the edge of the base as it bashed against the *Y* note. Nobody had been touching it.

"Old floors," Jasmine said, shifting her weight to make the wooden boards creak.

I leaned in to examine the board. "Or Trista telling us that Caleb didn't do it."

Lightning flashed, and I thought I saw faces outside the window, at the edge of the woods. Odd bulging eyes, like the aliens Wes used to mumble about in his sleep. Of course, as with all the other apparitions the house had thrown at me, they were gone the next moment, though the feeling of being stared at did not go away. Now, watching the glass wobble on the board with nobody touching it, I realized that perhaps the feeling never would go away.

"We should finish it," I said again, stronger this time.

Craig's face was still red, with a sheen of sweat. "Let's go beyond yes or no, then, shall we?" he said. He'd failed to properly keep the hair out of his eyes and a strand of it stuck to his forehead. "Honey, if you're really out there, or ... God forgive us ... *up there*, then help us settle this. Point to who took you away."

Silence as we watched the toppled glass wobble, perhaps because of the uneven floor, perhaps not.

The house creaked behind me. I expected another apparition, but it was only Marcus appearing in the doorway with a silver tray of steaming food—a type of casserole on rice, divided in the middle to separate the vegetarian side from the omnivore side. Caleb's head snapped up, as if he'd forgotten where he was.

The wine glass flew from the board, across the room, and directly at Marcus.

It shattered against the tray he carried. Shards of glass ejected in every direction as the tray clanged to the ground. Plates shattered, forks clanged, a perfect cube of tender beef left a trail of sauce as it tumbled across the rug.

Marcus hissed and clutched a bleeding hand.

"Daddy?" Jasmine said. Was she concerned for his injury, or for the possibility of his guilt?

"It was him," Ash said, pointing.

Blood dripped from Marcus's hand. He turned back to the kitchen, but Craig followed close behind him. "Marcus. Marcus! Don't you go far now. Ash, can you help me?"

Ash got up from his seat and trailed Marcus too, forming a barrier around him as he rushed to the kitchen, then held his hand under the sink faucet.

"Have you all lost your damn minds? A séance?"

"Did you do it, Marcus?" Craig asked.

"Of course I didn't do anything to Trista, Craig.

How long have we known each other? How long have we been *friends?*"

Ash pointed at the shattered glass sparkling in the firelight across the hall. "The glass pointed right at you. It's evidence."

"You fool," Marcus said as he wrapped his hand in a dish towel. "Kicking a glass at me is not *evidence*, and if we're at the point of throwing wild accusations, I have an idea of who kicked it."

"I saw it happen," Caleb mumbled.

"Saw *what* happ—" I began to ask him, but everyone was talking over each other.

Ash held an odd crooked smile on his face.

Marcus tightened the towel around his hand and ranted. "We've all seen it, Ash." He jabbed his wrapped hand in Ash's direction. Blood was already soaking through. The cut was bad. "The way you look at her. *Looked* at her, God damn it."

"Let me get this straight. You're accusing me now." Ash was as monotone as ever; if he was feeling anything, he kept it buried. "Accusing me of not only murdering someone you admit I care about, but staging a séance to kick a Ouija board and frame you. Do I have that right, Marcus? Because it sounds like a pretty complex plan, and have you ever heard of Occam's Razor?"

"You condescending piece of ..." Marcus said, and rushed around the kitchen counter toward Ash. Craig grabbed Marcus's arm and got an elbow rammed into his nose for it.

I watched in horror, but tried to hold on to the details and piece together what was happening. One piece that stood out was that Ash had been sitting a good distance from the Ouija board, and while I hadn't seen anyone kick it, there was no way Ash could have done it.

Marcus calmed down as soon as he saw Craig's bleeding nose. "Oh Craig, oh Christ, I'm sorry man." He grabbed another cotton dish towel from a drawer and held it to Craig's nose."

"It's fine," Craig said, but he recoiled from Marcus's touch and took the towel himself.

I cleared my throat. "Let's cool off. We still don't know anything here."

"I need a smoke," Marcus said.

Jasmine stepped forward. "I'll come with you, Dad."

Before Ash and Craig could object, I offered to go along and keep an eye on them. Nobody said anything, so I escorted the recently accused murderer to go have a cigarette and calm down.

The mud room near the stairs to the basement doubled as a smoking room, at least when the weather was bad. It smelled like cigarettes there before Marcus even lit his, and I could imagine generations of household help and rebellious teenagers using this one smelly room to get away from the odourless opulence of the rest of the house. A narrow door off the mud room must have led to the pantry near the family room—a clever layout to enable the hired help to load groceries right into the kitchen, or quickly slip outside to serve appetizers to the guests lounging at that tiki hut by the pool. That gave me another vision of grabbing a bottle of air freshener from the pantry to spray the mud room, in a futile attempt to hide their smoking habits from Craig.

Jasmine opened the back door while Marcus lit up. The sound of the storm was nearly deafening when it wasn't filtered through windows and walls, and I could feel the sting in my lungs from the acrid red rain. When lightning lit up the yard, I could see the swimming pool, the immaculately trimmed shrubbery all around the grounds, and the gated wall around the yard. Beyond that, towering, untamed trees loomed, reminding me that we were on an island of luxury in a sea of wilderness and chaos. Was it any wonder that some of the chaos had seeped inside?

Marcus tossed the cigarette outside after only a few puffs. He pulled two dish towels from under his shirt. "I didn't do this, Amy. I know you just met me and have no reason to believe me, but I didn't. I wouldn't. Why would I?"

Jasmine hugged him. "You treated her so well, Daddy. I know you didn't do it. Of course you didn't."

"If we can all just stay calm, we'll figure it out in the morning," I said.

But Marcus shook his head. He handed one of the towels to Jasmine, then grabbed an umbrella from a rack near the door. "If we cover our mouths it won't be too bad. Under umbrellas, running, our exposure time won't be too long, and we can make it to the car. I just had the filters replaced in Jasmine's car, so it will be safe in there."

"Wait," I said.

Jasmine helped Marcus wrap the towel around his face. He held up the increasingly red cloth failing to keep his hand from bleeding. "It's not safe for us here."

"You can't just *run away*," I said, my voice starting to crack. Because wasn't running away what I did best? Could I really protest this, when I'd left my entire family at the first sign of trouble?

"Look, you tried to keep us safe. I appreciate that— you coming all the way out here to fix our shit. But your room didn't keep Trista safe. You can't keep me and Jasmine safe now. You might not even be safe yourself. I had no part in this, which means one of the people back there did. You could come with us."

"No," I said. *I won't run away again.* "I won't try to stop you, but I need to see this through."

Jasmine touched my wrist. My lips trembled, and when she saw that I was about to break down, she leaned in and hugged me. "You remind me of Trista," she said, a tremble in her voice now too. "She always tackled problems head on."

Head on. Pretty much the opposite of the reality of my life, but I was something different to these people. These strangers. To anyone who didn't know me well, I was a stereotype, a fantasy.

I pulled back but held Jasmine at arm's reach a moment longer. "I'm so sorry about your friend. I'm going to do my best to help find justice for her."

Jasmine leaned close and spoke softly in my ear. "Oh, Amy, she wasn't just my friend."

Before I could ask what she meant, Marcus tied the cloth around her face and gently pushed her toward the door. "We gotta go now, honey."

They gave me one last wave as they slipped out through the open door, then ran across the path to a side gate where they could get out of the yard and around to Jasmine's car at the front of the house.

I started to think of excuses for letting them go. Did I even need any? This wasn't my family. None of this was in my job description.

A loud crack rang out, accompanied by a flash. I went to close the door against the thunder, but there was something wrong—the flash didn't have the red tinge of the storm's lightning, the crack wasn't booming like thunder.

Jasmine screamed.

I swung the door back open, and then a double-flash

of lightning lit up the yard. Marcus lay on the ground. Jasmine covered him with outstretched arms.

Behind them, a tall person wearing a gas mask lowered a rifle. "We warned you," he shouted over the thrashing storm. "Now it's our turn."

PART III
AN INVASION

CHAPTER 7

I panicked, and in that moment of weakness, I was stupid enough to try something heroic. They needed their fantasy. Their Jack. The one who didn't run from her problems.

Two umbrellas were left in the rack by the door. I grabbed the larger one, flipped open the Velcro strap with my thumb like it was the safety on a gun, then pushed the trigger on the handle as I ran out the door. The umbrella whooshed open. Instead of putting it over my head to block out the rain, I held it in front of me. Was I thinking that it would block a bullet? Perhaps my panicked mind thought so.

It would, at least, make it harder to aim at me. Another crack filled the air, and I didn't feel any pain, so I kept running and hoped Jasmine and Marcus would still be breathing when I reached them.

The wind tugged at the umbrella. Rain splattered at

my face. I could feel the sting as droplets exploded on my skin, and my lungs burned from the horrible mist that filled the air when it rained, ever since the day of the first environmental catastrophe—the same day I lost my family. The smell of the mist, which I thought of as rotten apples, and others associated with licorice, or old molasses, was strong enough to make me retch. I didn't have long before the rain would make me sick for days, or worse.

I wasn't sure how many bullets that rifle could fire, but surely he'd need to reload. Where was Mae? She would know. And she had a gun of her own.

Nobody else saw Mae, I thought. *They all looked at me strangely when I brought her up. Could I have dreamed her up when I bumped my head?*

I nearly stumbled on Jasmine and Marcus. The rain and darkness were so thick that I could hardly see them, but I heard Marcus groan. That meant he was alive, but I could make out a lot of red.

Jasmine faced me. "You came?"

There was no time to verbalize a plan. I lay my umbrella down in front of us for cover, jamming it in the branches of a rose bush beside the path so it wouldn't blow away immediately. I did the same with Marcus's umbrella.

I pointed back at the glowing entrance to the house, where I must have dropped my flashlight as I bolted. "Too much light. We'd be sitting ducks."

Jasmine pointed at where the path split off to the

right, then across the darkened pool deck, and over to another entrance that must have been near the ball room.

"What about the cellar door?" I asked.

Jasmine shook her head. "There ain't no cellar door. We only joked about it when we were kids. How ... how did you know that?"

Mae had said she got in through a cellar door. How did she get in the basement?

No time.

Marcus sat up. I took Jasmine's umbrella and she got an arm around him, while I helped him from the other side. We all coughed, a last chance to get it out, then I held a finger up to my lips, and we bolted along the path.

One of the umbrellas I'd put on the ground blew free and sailed toward the large man in the gas mask— Mary Poppins on the offensive.

It was enough distraction for us to break free of the meagre light from the door and enter the darkness of the back deck. Surely he wouldn't be able to see us there unless the lightning gave us away. Jasmine tried to keep the last umbrella over us as we ran, but the stinging water still got in my face, and I could barely draw enough breath to keep running. Marcus wheezed too, and I hoped it was only because of the rain and not a bullet through his lung.

I glanced back, but there was no sign of the man in the gas mask. Lighting flashed in the distance and, still, he did not appear, which I hoped meant he'd lost track of us too.

The pool did not have a fence around it. *That's not up to provincial safety codes. What if a kid wandered away and fell in?* Apparently part of my mind was always at work, worrying about government codes and child safety, even when I was being shot at.

Jasmine led us around the pool carefully. In the dark, it was nearly invisible, but she knew what to look for. I hoped—and perhaps Jasmine was hoping the same thing—that the man behind us would fail to notice the pool before tumbling in and drowning.

We crossed the pool deck, then the bit of lawn before the other back entrance.

I heard a voice behind us. "Shit!" I hoped for a splash following that, but none came. Still, if he came at the pool from the wrong angle, it would take a moment to get around it, which would buy us more time.

An APT Security sign was poked into the garden beside the back entrance, identical to the one around front: *This house protected by APT Security.* A security camera above it would have backed up the sign's promise, at least when power and communications were functional. I'd approved the design for the signs myself, back when I was more involved with the marketing department at APT. One feature I'd insisted on was a long, sturdy stake to go in the ground—if homeowners had to replace the sign too often, or neighbours saw broken signs blowing across the lawn, it'd do immeasurable harm to our brand.

I grabbed the sign and pulled, taking just a bit of pride in the fact that I had to apply significant force to wrest it from the wet earth.

"The key. My front pocket," Marcus said.

"It's okay, I've got mine," Jasmine said as she produced a handful of keys from her purse and unlocked the back door. How many people had keys to this house?

Splashing footsteps approached from the left. I didn't even see the man until he was upon us, suddenly blinding us with a flashlight.

"Get in the house!" he shouted, his voice muffled.

Marcus collapsed through the doorway. Jasmine followed and cushioned his fall, dragging him inside. When I hesitated, the man roughly grabbed my shoulder and turned me around, then pushed me toward the door.

"G-go! Now."

Thunder crashed, and anger flashed within me. Was this the same guy that was shooting at us? His voice sounded different, less certain. But he could have a gun too. He could follow us inside and use it at any moment.

I knew a sturdy lawn sign would protect my company's brand from immeasurable harm, but this was even better: my brand could do immeasurable harm to this asshole's face. I lunged backward with the pointy end. He screeched and dropped the flashlight.

In the light reflecting off the ground, I could finally see who was terrorizing us. He wore a full raincoat that may have been yellow at one point, but the red rain pouring over it had dyed it orangey-pink. His gas mask, too, had a bleached pink hue, and now it also had a puncture just below the left eyepiece, with my APT security sign sticking out of it.

He removed the sign and tossed it to the ground.

"Who are you?" I shouted at him. "Why did you kill Trista?"

He clawed at his face. Blood dribbled from the rip in the mask before the rain washed it away.

"Why did you kill Trista?" I asked again, picking up the sign and pointing it at him like a spear.

Finally, he raised his head. I could just make out blue eyes behind the glass windows in the gas mask. "Who the f-fuck is Trista?"

He went for a pocket in his raincoat.

Gun. Gun! Gun! my mind reminded me. I threw myself backward and slammed the door shut before I could find out if my mind was correct.

Jasmine was hyperventilating. "Who the hell was that? What is happening?"

I snapped the lock on the door shut, then looked for a chain lock. No dice. "I don't know," I said.

"Oh, Daddy." Jasmine sobbed. Marcus mumbled

something. His breath came out in an unsteady rhythm.

Voices shouted on the other side of the door. As I'd suspected, there were two of them. The glass window in the door was too high for me to see out of, but beams of light suggested a pair of bobbing flashlights carried by the two men: the big guy with the rifle, and the smaller guy in the pink raincoat.

"We need to get away from the door and warn the others."

Jasmine closed her eyes and exhaled slowly, willing herself to calm down. She unwrapped the cloth from her face and applied it to Marcus's wound, which was forming a pool on the tile floor of the small anteroom we'd found ourselves in. "Yes. Yes, okay. Daddy, can you walk?" She grabbed his good hand and placed it on the cloth. "Put pressure on this. It'll help."

"I can walk. I'm fine," Marcus said in clipped breaths.

But that wound was in his left side, just below his chest, dangerously close to his heart and even closer to his lungs.

We stumbled back into the main hallway, coming out near the ball room. When we all stopped coughing for a moment, the house was silent, as if nothing had just happened.

We passed the alcove leading to a room that looked like the lobby of a movie theatre. A blinking light from some kind of speaker—obviously battery-operated—lit up the dormant popcorn machine, and I allowed myself a moment to realize how hungry I was.

"You know my dad didn't have anything to do with this, right?" Jasmine asked.

"Honey—" Marcus said.

I interrupted. "I know, I know. It's their fault. Whoever those people outside are, it's *their* fault. Trista, the strange noises, the flying wine glass—maybe they poisoned us, somehow. Made us hallucinate. It must have been those men all along."

Jasmine wouldn't make eye contact with me. "Yeah. Maybe."

I stopped, forcing all of us to stop, since Jasmine and I were practically carrying Marcus between us. "What do you mean *maybe?*"

Her gaze darted up the hall, where we were headed. "Caleb has been sitting by the windows, watching the lane to the house. Sometimes he watches the back paths. He says odd things about what's out there. Sometimes he mumbles to himself when he thinks no one else is in the room. He … he almost acts like he knew this was going to happen."

I thought of what the man in the pink raincoat had said: *Who the fuck is Trista?* "What are you saying?"

She nudged us forward. Marcus winced as she propped him up. "I'm not necessarily saying anything. Just … just let's keep an eye on Caleb."

Sure enough, Caleb was in his usual position peeking through the curtains of the family room. Craig manned his own window across the hall in the kitchen. Both of them jumped when I coughed to announce our presence.

"Watch out, he's back," Ash said, raising his hands a little too dramatically. He'd been cleaning the food and shattered glass from the floor.

"He's been shot, you asshole," Jasmine said.

Craig rushed into the hallway to help take some of Marcus's weight from us. "We heard the shots outside. Ash thought it was Marcus pulling something, but ..."

"Pulling something? You're still listening to this idiot?" Marcus said. "Two men in gas masks are out there, with guns. Yeah, those were gunshots, so stay away from the windows, okay? You people are so damn white."

We propped Marcus against the hallway wall, out of the line of sight of any windows. With his weight off of me and a moment to catch my breath, I realized how *hard* it was to breathe. I'd only been in the storm for two or three minutes, but it was the largest dose of the environmental catastrophe I'd exposed myself to since the beginning, and the storms were less severe back then. My lungs screamed, like the first and only time I'd tried weed. My skin itched, too, but I knew scratching would only make it worse.

"First aid?" I asked between coughs.

Caleb stood up to get medical supplies.

I pointed at Caleb. "Someone should go with him."

"Jesus, fine, Ash, will you go with him?" Craig said. He crouched beside Marcus, shaking with nerves. "What happened out there?"

We told him, and it seemed to convince him that there had been a horrible misunderstanding. Marcus didn't murder Trista, and the real enemies were outside with guns, likely intent on getting in and robbing the place. And on top of all that, séances weren't real.

But if robbery was the motive, why would they lock Trista in the safe room, kill her, then go back outside? If they had locked her in the room while the rest of the family was away, wouldn't *that* be the perfect time for a robbery? It made no sense.

Ash returned with a first aid kit, which he tossed at Craig's feet.

"Where's Caleb?" Craig asked.

"He freaked out. Said he needed to protect Trista. I told him, *too late*, but then he said he meant he had to find the crowbar he left by the safe room. I think he's lost it. And I'm being charitable by assuming he ever had it."

I crawled to the kitchen. The curtains were closed, so the risk of getting sniped from outside was low, but I could see bobbing lights backlighting the fabric. They were still out there. I put the security sign down on the counter of the kitchen island, then returned to the hall to help patch up Marcus. "Do you have any guns?" I asked Craig.

He shook his head. "Of course we don't have any guns."

"Axes? Tools? Anything?"

Craig held up Marcus's shirt while Jasmine cleaned his wound. She whimpered as she did it, but I had to give her credit for keeping it together, not vomiting or losing control entirely.

Marcus cleared his throat, and when he spoke his voice sounded thin, like he was working with half an air supply. "The outdoor tools would do some damage. But they're out in the back of the tiki shed."

That thatched-roof hut across the pool deck, where those bobbing lights outside came from. There was no way I'd go back out there. "Damn," I said.

Craig shook his head and his eyes watered. "This is what the safe room was for. We could have waited it out in there."

"Not an option now, Craig," Ash said. "If we didn't have Marcus with us, we could make a run for it. Have we forgotten that he's the one who made the safe room unusable by stuffing it with your daughter's body?"

Marcus just shook his head sadly, but I could almost feel the heat coming off of Jasmine. I backed away, feeling awkward, or even unsafe, hovering in the middle of these people.

Jasmine shook as she held gauze to her father's wound. "Still? You *still* think Dad did this? *Why* would he do anything to Trista? You're the one who's been obsessed with her since she was, what, fifteen years old? Nobody else will say it, but we all thought it was you." She inhaled through bared teeth. "I guarantee, the moment we saw Trista on that screen, everybody in this family wondered where you were when it happened."

For the first time, I noticed Ash express emotion. His lips sucked inward and tightened, his fist clenched. Was it embarrassment? Or anger? He composed himself a second later. "Well then you must have been greatly disappointed when you realized I was talking with you when it happened."

I backed away further. I needed something to hold on to, something certain. I turned to the kitchen counter and reached for my security stake.

It wasn't there.

"Yes, you were with me," Jasmine said. "Which is why I'm blaming the God damn men with guns outside instead of continuing to throw out accusations in here."

I crouched to search the floor, because surely the sign had just slid off the kitchen counter as I'd placed it there in my messy state of mind, but in the shadows of the flickering candlelight, I could barely see anything, and as I pawed around I couldn't feel anything either.

Dammit. I needed a weapon, in case anything else happened. Like if any of the men managed to get inside.

Like from the door I'd left open when I ran to help

Marcus and Jasmine. The door just on the other side of the kitchen pantry ...

"Oh no," I whispered.

I grasped the edge of the counter to pull myself up. Slowly, slowly, slowly I peeked over the edge of the kitchen island until I could see the pantry door.

Behind the door's frosted glass, two light patches could have been mistaken for a pair of mugs on a high shelf. But then the two orbs turned toward each other, coalescing into the gas mask's alien-like approximation of a face.

I ducked back behind the counter. "Guys," I whispered as loud as I could, but they were still shouting at each other behind me. "Go!" I shouted as I stood up. "Run!"

The pantry door swung open, and the man pointed his gun at me.

CHAPTER 8

"*R*un!" I screamed again, then leaped out of the kitchen, into the hallway. My legs carried me without any effort on my part. They were attached to me, part of me, but it wasn't me moving those legs, just pure fight-or-flight panic.

I was carried toward the end of the hall, and once there, I'd have a choice. Up or down. A moment's hesitation and I'd feel the bullet ripping through my lungs, I knew it. Just like poor Marcus. Up was stupid. It was always the stupid girl who went up the stairs, trapping herself in the house.

I was halfway downstairs before I realized the basement was just as much of a trap. Hadn't it already done that job once today?

Stupid, stupid, stupid.

The open basement where the safe room was located

wouldn't leave many places to hide, so I turned before I got there, ducking into another hallway, then another room. My shoulder rammed into a shelf. I used the dim light of my cell phone screen to determine where I was. Jars full of a dark substance rattled against each other, jingling away my location. More carefully now, I stepped around tall shelves filled with jars, boxes, and toys. I went a row deeper into the room; these shelves housed ancient computers, tools, and other antique gadgets that the tech guys at work would kill to pick through.

Something scraped the pavement behind me.

I squatted. Shit. He'd heard me.

One of them heard you. One of the two, I reminded myself, making sure not to underestimate the trouble I was in.

I crawled behind some boxes on the bottom shelf and turned off my phone. Quietly, quietly, quietly, I inched further along the row, in case he'd spotted me hiding.

A flashlight scanned the room, with slivers of its light bursting through gaps in the shelves' contents to create glowing shafts in the dusty air.

He stepped into the room.

I crawled around the edge of the shelf behind me, slipping back another row, trapping myself deeper. The flashlight bobbed, and his footsteps drew closer.

I searched for a weapon. Something that could be used as a weapon. Anything. This shelf was only boxes.

The next one over was piles of folded clothing. The next—

I gasped and jumped back. Black eyes and gnashing teeth glowed in one of the shafts of light approaching behind me. I thought the dog had reappeared, but no, this time a bear had burst through from the other side of the shelf.

I scrambled backward. My hand fell onto something roughly cylindrical. I grabbed it from the shelf and held it in front of me, but the bear stayed where it was.

The man rounded the corner. I held my new weapon in front of me—a knife! I'd managed to stumble upon a knife.

The flashlight's beam was blinding. It turned to illuminate the bear.

"We used to play Goldilocks and the Three Bears." It was Caleb's soft voice. He turned the flashlight to illuminate two more bear heads, sitting on the shelf beside the first one. They were only masks, but the eyes and the teeth were frighteningly realistic. "Dad would be one bear, Uncle Marcus would be another, and I felt so special when they let me be the third bear. Trista and Jasmine took turns being Goldilocks, pretending to sleep in her castle while we snuck up on her with our masks on and startled her. Trista was best at playing her. She'd scream so loud, then laugh and laugh and laugh."

He lowered the flashlight. His eyes were puffy and red. In his other hand, he held the rusty crowbar he'd used in his attempt to pry Trista out of the safe room. "I keep thinking she's going to wake up," he said.

I took a step back.

"Bears used to make me happy," he said, caressing the bear masks on the shelf. "I wonder if they will any more. Dogs used to make me happy too, until Dad's story about the one in the ball room. Now I hear dogs howling in the woods when I'm scared."

I swallowed the lump in my throat and willed my heart to stop beating. "Caleb. We need to keep our voices down and turn the light off. Those men have gotten into the house."

He tightened his grip on the crowbar, then set the flashlight down. It cast dark shadows under his already-dark eyes, and I didn't like him being so close, his crowbar vibrating with pent-up anxiety. I gripped the knife tighter. "Where are they?" he asked.

"Right above us, far as I know. But one of them saw me come down here."

"Is everyone okay?" he asked, still not whispering, still too loud.

"Shhh. I don't know."

His hand shot out, reaching for my knife. I jerked, and the knife jabbed his hand. He giggled like a little boy, then impaled himself again and stepped back. "I played with *that* as a kid too."

I touched the tip of the knife. It bounced up and down on a spring, the plastic blade retreating down into the plastic handle. "Your fucking toys are going to give me a heart attack," I said.

He giggled again. I couldn't help but smile.

"Come on," I said. "We need to protect ourselves, and maybe all these toys will help. Wanna play Goldilocks again?"

We chatted quietly while we worked. As Caleb opened up, he seemed so *innocent,* in the sense that all children are innocent. Yet I couldn't let go of the thought that someone from the house could still be involved in his sister's death—after all, the man in the pale pink raincoat had asked: *Who the fuck is Trista?* Plus, innocent children are capable of some horribly guilty things, so what the fuck does that word, *innocent,* really mean anyway?

He got moody again when we grabbed some materials from the central room. The one with Trista's tomb in it.

Like I'd always done when Todd was miserable, I distracted him. "Caleb, is there a cellar door around here? One that leads outside? It's how Mae said she got in, but Jasmine said there isn't one."

His head snapped up. "How did you know about that? We talked about it all the time. We saw in some old movie we all watched together—Donnie Darko, I think?—that *cellar door* is the most beautiful phrase in the English language. Not because of what it means, but just the way it rolls off the tongue, you know?"

"Cellar door," I said, too loud, then quieted my voice back to a whisper. "Cellar door, cellar door, cellar door. Yeah, okay, I see it."

"So we joked about it all the time, thinking of excuses for saying it. 'Time to go inside? Let's take the cellar door!' You know?"

"But there's not actually another door to the basement?"

"Nah."

"So how did Mae get in?"

He scrunched up his face and studied mine, like he was trying to decide if I could be trusted. The feeling was mutual. "You really saw Mae?"

I sighed. "Okay, so to tell the truth, I'd just hit my head pretty bad, and I ... I possibly hallucinated seeing a big dog right before that. But I saw her. How would I even know who she was otherwise? How would I even know her name?"

Caleb opened his mouth to say something, but nothing came out.

"I know it sounds crazy."

He shrugged. "We all go a little mad sometimes. Isn't that a line from some fairy tale?"

I could live with that. We quickly walked back toward the staircase, which was the only *real* entrance to the basement, carrying armfuls of materials for our little project. I'd gotten inspiration for this project from my husband, Wes, when he had broken his foot just before he went missing forever (*but left the car in the driveway,* my mind liked to remind me whenever I thought about him). We put the materials down, then headed for the nearby room. The one with the bouncy castle that had so freaked me out earlier.

Heavy footsteps stomped directly above us.

Caleb finally remembered to whisper. "Mae hasn't been here in a while. But I remember her. She told such great stories, and really knew the history of them. Once, she came with her gun—she's a cop, you know—and that scared me when I was a kid. But she also dressed so funny that I couldn't *really* be scared. Not of her, anyway."

An idea came to me. Call it troubleshooting, like when a customer had a problem with their safe room system, and I'd tell them various steps to try out. Sometimes I'd tell them to do something that I *knew* wouldn't work, but their ability to carry out the instructions and report back would tell me about the person. The person was just as important as the technology.

"I noticed she dressed funny. Her big orange hat with the rose on it."

Caleb giggled hysterically. "Her orange hat, yeah."

We continued with our project, hurrying, knowing that those men could come down the stairs at any moment. The bouncy castle was heavy, and even with Caleb's help laying it out across the hall, sweat dripped down the back of my neck. My heart still raced from fear, but it was joined by a sort of pride; as Mae had said, this family needed their hero, and I was the only one with the qualifications for that role at the moment.

"Goldilocks time?" Caleb said.

"That's right. If Goldilocks didn't want those bears coming in, she should've rigged up some security."

Caleb giggled again, covering his mouth so it wasn't too loud. "Amy, it was Goldilocks breaking into the bears' house."

I kicked our new security rig to make sure it was solid. It was simple, but it would hold up. It would hurt. I wiped the sweat from my brow and flicked it aside. "Well, then I guess that makes us the bears."

A door creaked open. The sound carried through the walls, seeped into the floor, then shot into the basement in such a way that it sounded like it was nearby, though I could not determine exactly where in the house the door was located.

A moment later, someone yelped, then the stomping of several pairs of feet travelled across the house. The footsteps faded in volume quickly, presumably as the chase led to the second floor.

"I think that was Jasmine," Caleb whispered from across the hallway, crouched in the doorway to the shelf room.

I nodded. My hands shook as I tried to find a good place to put them. If the men upstairs didn't kill me, the anxiety from waiting for them to arrive would. I couldn't figure out the motives of the pair of men; was it robbery? Murder? Worse? What did *OUR TURN* mean? But in any case, they'd search the basement at some point, and that's when this rough plan would bounce into place.

I should have looked for a weapon, but was there time now? Or would I feel that bullet tear apart my insides as soon as I let my guard down?

More doors creaked open on the floor above. The sounds seemed to be getting closer, but it was difficult to tell. That last thump could have been a footstep, or it could have been distant thunder.

Another thump was definitely in the house, less muffled than before. Somebody was coming down the stairs.

Thump, thump, thump as heavy boots hit each step. It was definitely one of the men. Only Jasmine, Marcus, and I were wearing shoes from our excursion outside, and the other two were either on the second floor or bleeding to death.

A flashlight lit up the corridor. It cast odd patterns of shadow from the irregular, deflated bouncy castle that we'd laid on the concrete floor of the hallway. I remembered my insane thought that the castle was alive with hungry rats underneath, and the shadows now writhing across its surface brought that thought to life. Except now I welcomed it. That particular fantasy had been recruited to my side.

I leaned back into the room so the man wouldn't spot me.

His footsteps stomped closer. His voice sounded loud in the dark: "C-come on out, little girl. L-little boy too. You d-down here?" While he tried to project his voice, it wavered and stuttered as if he was cold, though surely he was only scared. This was the same man who attacked us on the way into the house, who I'd jabbed in the face. With the pink coat and the gas mask like a little cylindrical nose, I began to think of him as a piggy.

"Little g-girl!" He coughed, which made me want to do the same, with my lungs still stinging from exposure to the outdoors. "I've got a present for you!" Metal tapped against metal; I could picture the handgun I knew he had, tapping against his flashlight.

His boot squeaked as he took his first step onto the castle. "What the fuck," he muttered, but he kept moving. Another squeak. Soon the trap would spring, and he'd be running out the door, never to come back. *Just like in that movie Home Alone,* I'd said to Caleb while we put the trap together, and he didn't say anything, but from his half-disappointed expression I knew he was thinking about how the robbers in Home Alone kept coming even after Macaulay Culkin sprung all his traps.

Another squeak. How was he getting so far?

He drew close. Soon he'd be across the bouncy castle. He'd round the corner, pull the trigger, and I'd be dead in an instant.

There was no way out of here. No cellar door behind me, nothing to defend myself with. Except …

He took another step, and his boot hit concrete. He'd managed to avoid our trap. It was either extraordinary luck, or somehow he'd seen through it.

I was out of options. It was time to tackle this problem *head on*, like Jasmine said Trista always did.

I sprung from the doorway, with the knife raised. The plastic knife with the spring in it. But he didn't know that.

It was enough to make him recoil. He raised his right hand, but he was already stepping backward, and the undulating folds of the bouncy castle seemed to reach for his feet. He went down sideways, trying to steady himself, but tripping again on one of the bricks we'd placed under the castle.

He landed on his back, and from the howl of pain, I knew he'd hit the right spot—one of the boards we'd put under the rubber, lined with rusty, corrugated nails that were now embedded in his back.

I leapt at him with the knife before he had time to raise his gun again, but I hesitated for a split second, perhaps out of fear, or perhaps distantly realizing that the charade would be over if he felt the plastic blade up close. My hesitation left him with time to dodge, but as he rolled to the side, his wrist encountered another row of nails.

The gun tumbled to the side. Rivulets of blood trickled through the folds and creases of the castle like little waggling rat tails.

"You c-c-c—" he stammered.

"Caleb! Time to go!" I shouted as I regained my footing and kicked the gun away from the man's reach.

I grabbed the gun and tossed the plastic knife onto the man's chest. It was so light it seemed to float through the air before clacking against his rubber rain-coat. Caleb emerged, carrying his crowbar more like a baby than a weapon.

The man kicked and howled as he attempted to remove his impaled wrist from the undulating rubber. *Squeal, piggy.* Caleb ducked past me, away from his reach, only stepping on the castle's blue-painted windows, which we'd designated as safe areas.

I only took my eyes off the man for a second to aim my own steps, but he moved fast, grabbing my ankle with his free hand. I went down. My knee hit the corner of one of the bricks under the rubber, and it made a very bad sound as I felt something snap out of place inside my kneecap.

I kicked forward, aiming for a window. The man held on for a moment, but he was still impaled. He let go when the hole in his wrist elongated, gushing more blood.

Jesus.

I hopped once, twice, and then I was on the other side of the castle. I aimed the gun at him. Behind his gas mask, marred by the rip where I'd jabbed him outside, wild, frightened blue eyes looked up at me. "What do you want?" I cried.

"W-what do you think? The house."

I tried to keep the gun steady, but the pain in my knee was making my arms weak too. "And the girl?"

"The daughter? Tell her to keep away."

Once again, he denied any knowledge of Trista, didn't even know she was down the hall, dead. Everything suddenly felt colder. The gun in my hand was ice. "She doesn't have the luxury of keeping away now. But you will."

"It's—it's ours. The house. It doesn't belong to you anymore," he said. The grey walls of the rubber castle around him had turned red with smudged blood.

I flipped the safety off. "It never did, buddy, but now I'm the one with the gun. I'd say that makes me king of the castle."

He laughed. "You weren't supposed to be here. I don't know who you are, lady, but maybe you get it."

He tried to get up again, wincing in pain.

Something thumped upstairs.

"Let's go!" Caleb said. And of course, we did have to go. I couldn't shoot this man just because I had the gun. I turned and tried climbing the stairs, but it was like a rock was embedded in my knee, preventing me from straightening it. Caleb practically had to drag me with his skinny arms. We jammed a chair under the handle of the door at the top of the stairs, which would at least delay the man down there.

The house seemed eerily silent. I thought I could hear breathing, somewhere, but as always, it could have been sounds from outside, muffled by the thick walls. Or it could have been a ghost. But what I knew for sure was that one of the men who thought they owned the place was still wandering around inside, and it was time for him to get the fuck out.

CHAPTER 9

"*D*on't cry baby, don't cry, don't cry," Paul Simon sang.

The power had flashed on, and for just a moment, I'd seen the house as the family thought of it—bright, inviting, somehow more modern—before it went dark again. The power flash must have also reset the speaker in the lobby to the movie room and set it playing, because now Paul Simon was singing Boy in the Bubble. The droning accordion and uncommon South African cadence took on a menacing tone echoing in the dark, as if coming from somewhere further than down the hall. Somewhere further than Africa. When Paul Simon sang about distant, dying constellations, then pleaded his final "don't cry," there was a brief pause, then the song started again.

"This is Dad's music," Caleb said.

"You don't say! This is the ultimate dad music. It

doesn't surprise me one bit that Craig would rock out to this."

Caleb chuckled. "He used to listen to it over and over, when we were kids. Sometimes he still does. Trista and me make fun of him for it all the time. I hated this song. I don't really hate it right now though."

"Well, at least it makes for a password you can remember. That didn't keep you from writing it down anyway though, did it?"

DONT CRY DONT CRY. It was written on the sticky note on the fridge. Caleb didn't seem to get what I was saying, so he just remained silent, which was probably for the best as we slowly searched each room, talking quietly enough that the music would drown out our approach. My heart raced and the pain in my knee introduced some delirium to my pounding head, though, and ideas raced so quickly in my mind that I couldn't keep them inside. "It's a Bluetooth speaker playing the dad rock?"

"Yeah."

"The power surge must have brought it to life. It might not be long before we have light. And cell service. Then I can call in for the failsafe password, and we can find out what happened to Trista."

Caleb stopped. His hand on my arm had been helping me limp along, but now it squeezed harder than it needed to. "*They* did. You believe they killed her, don't you?" My heart leaped. Jasmine's last words to me returned: *let's keep an eye on Caleb*. Now his watery eyes focused intently on me, twinkling in the light of the candles that still burned around the kitchen.

"Sure," I said. Dammit, I couldn't keep my thoughts inside, even if it would turn Caleb against me, maybe even anger him. But I still had the gun. "On second thought, no. No. I mentioned Trista to the man downstairs twice, and both times he denied knowing anything about her."

"They're killers. Monsters. Of course they'd deny it." Caleb's voice was cold.

"They tried to kill Marcus, tried to kill us, they've broken into your house. What reason would they have to deny one more crime?"

"I don't know, but I've seen this coming. I showed you that note. 'Abandon this place.' They warned us, and they've been around here for months. Did you know that? I saw them before, when they came up here in a white truck. Everyone else was out, so they thought nobody was home. They watched the house for half an hour, and I watched them from an upstairs window. Nobody believed me, but I've been watching for them ever since. Sometimes I don't sleep. Sometimes I'll see that white truck out there in the woods at night."

I shivered. I thought I'd seen a truck in the woods on the way in, but dismissed it as an illusion, a phantom, just tired eyes making things up. I couldn't rule out the possibility that Caleb was imagining things too

—or lying—but a few too many coincidences were starting to line up. I urged him to ease me down into one of the chairs in the family room. I needed to rest for a moment, but it also allowed me to concentrate on monitoring the dark around us, in case our voices had attracted any attention. When I saw and heard nothing except the music, I lowered my voice and continued prodding. "It still doesn't make any sense to me. They came and snuck in, without anyone noticing, killed your sister, then left, then came back *later* to kill us?"

"I don't know."

"And how did she get in the safe room in the first place?"

"She was on a tour of universities," Caleb said. "Did you know? She didn't come with me and Dad to go see my aunt, which made Dad a bit sour. She was supposed to come home at the same time as us, but she must have gotten home early, and someone put her in that … that place."

"Okay, so they came when they thought the house was empty, but Trista was here. Why would they lock her in the room though?" I was only thinking out loud now.

Caleb's nostrils twitched. Against Paul Simon's wishes, he was going to cry. "I don't know, okay?"

"Neither do I. That's all I'm trying to say. We can't assume that they're guilty, and we can't assume anyone else is innocent. Where were you when your sister was … attacked?"

131

He looked like he'd been slapped. Then he reconsidered, and his eyes searched the room, as if he were seeing into the past. "Fine. I was here. I was alone … Dad wasn't feeling well, so he said he was going to bed. Marcus was cleaning up. I dunno where Ash went. I think I dozed off, then … then a minute later … I heard the scream … and—" He trailed off and buried his face in his hands, sobbing.

"Shhh!" I said, and it came out more like *shut the fuck up* than *there there*, so I tried again, cautiously stroking his wavy hair: "shhhhh, don't cry."

It seemed to calm him. The hair-stroking maneuver had worked with Todd too. Now I wanted to cry.

He sniffled. The candles behind him emphasized the round edges of his face, and how young he looked. He must've been … what? Seventeen? I'd thought of him as much older than Todd had been, but there were only a few years between them. If Todd had lived, he'd have been Caleb's age soon. And like Todd, I had trouble believing Caleb could hurt anyone even if he wanted to.

I must have been looking at him strangely, because he stopped crying and withdrew into the shadows. After a few moments of silence, he changed the subject. "Did you actually see Mae?"

"Yes."

"So where is she?" Now he was interrogating me. Perhaps he even suspected me when it came to Trista. I was the outsider here, after all. It wasn't *my* family. Mine was gone.

"I don't know where she went. I think she's fine, though; she's gotta be, right? We would have heard something otherwise, like a shout, or a gunshot." I reached out and put a hand on Caleb's knee, and looked him straight in the eye. "Mae's waiting for the right moment, okay? She seems to know what she's doing."

We sat there for a few more minutes, catching our breath, preparing for what came next. I took stock of what we had. The gun felt heavy in my lap and I almost wished I had my plastic knife back. They served the same purpose, after all: convince others that you're dangerous. I would never *use* the gun, so it was an empty threat, like the knife. Like fairy tales—stories we tell ourselves to convince us there's hope, that we have control. *Mae's waiting for the right moment.*

Like the security company lawn signs, which anyone could buy online for fifteen bucks, even if you don't have a security system, because just convincing the bad guys you're dangerous to them is enough. Except, that hadn't worked today, had it? No, the world had flipped. Even unspoken rules no longer applied.

Something thumped against the floor down the hall.

"Give me the gun?" Caleb said.

I shook my head. I'd convinced myself that he didn't kill Trista, but there was still something I didn't trust about him. Instead, I gestured for him to help me out of my chair, and I limped as quietly as I could toward the source of the noise.

Another sound came from the dining room just off the foyer—the raspy whisper of a living thing rubbing against the inorganic house around it. I pointed the gun at the French doors. Through the gemlike pattern of the glass, I saw only dark fragments of the room beyond.

I jutted my chin toward the door. Caleb got the hint and swung it open, then stepped back as I turned on my flashlight. Chair coverings looked like shrouds over upright corpses, and I almost pulled the trigger before realizing the room was devoid of life.

There was a closet.

Was that the clearing of a throat inside? Or was I only hearing the rain gurgling in the gutters, interpreting the mechanistic movements of nature as the work of a conscious being?

I realized that somebody had stopped the Bluetooth speaker down the hall behind us. Paul Simon had been silenced. It hadn't been playing long enough for the battery to have run out.

Something shifted in the closet. Either someone was hiding in there, or the house really did have rats. I gestured at Caleb again, and although his hands shook, he reached toward the closet's doorknob and yanked it open.

I nearly shot Craig. He shouted in fear—only a sharp bark before he realized it was us, but loud enough that it echoed in the now-silent house, and would surely attract the attention of the intruder. And if that didn't do it, Craig's round of coughs surely would. When he regained his breath, he put his arms around Caleb.

"We need to go," I said.

"Thank God you're okay," Craig said to his son.

"I'm fine."

Craig ruffled Caleb's curly hair and he gingerly gripped his son's chin between his thumb and fore-finger to move his head from side to side, looking him over, as if examining both sides of his head would result in a medical diagnosis. The little gesture tickled something in my brain. *Remember this*, I thought. *Remember this gesture.*

Caleb pulled away from his dad's grip. "Have you seen anyone else? Mae?"

"No sign of Mae." Craig briefly looked at me. He was still skeptical about Mae even having been here.

"Let's go. Now," I said.

Suddenly the house was alive with sound. From the basement, the trapped intruder pounded on the door and shouted for help. Heavy footsteps stomped from the other side of the house—footsteps that could only have come from the other guy's heavy boots.

"New plan: back in the closet," I whispered. We piled in, then I closed the door as quietly as I could. Craig clamped his hand over his mouth and his head jerked as he tried to suppress his coughing, but his breath still hissed as it escaped his nose.

The footsteps passed us, headed toward the basement. This was our chance.

We got back into the hallway, then ran to the foyer. The footsteps behind us stopped. Silence for a moment. Then he turned and stomped back toward us.

We couldn't risk the rain, especially with Craig's lungs already about to give out. "Up the stairs!"

We climbed, no longer caring about the noise we made. When Craig realized my knee was injured, he helped as best he could, and his skinny arms around my waist were somehow reassuring. At the top, I looked over the railing, and nearly fumbled the gun, sending it tumbling to the foyer's tile floor. The intruder who had shot Marcus stood there. The big guy, wearing a jet black hazard suit below his gas mask. If the one in the pink rain coat was a piggy, this one was a black bear.

He grunted and stomped toward the steps, probably not even aware that I had his friend's gun shakily trained on him, but before he began to climb, Marcus leapt from under the stairs and ran straight for him.

The two men—poppa bear Marcus and the invading black bear—became a blur as they struggled. The intruder was bigger, but Marcus was stronger, and soon the man was pinned to the floor. His rifle was strapped to his back, now jammed underneath him. Marcus's weight wouldn't hold him for long.

"Marcus! Take this!" I shouted down. I tossed the handgun to him, and miraculously, he caught it.

"You stay down. I will not hesitate to use this," Marcus said, pushing the gun hard against the intruder's temple. I believed him. In his hands, the weapon was no fairy tale. This story, finally, was coming to an end.

Except Marcus's hands were shaky, and he swayed like he was a tree about to topple.

"We need to help him," Craig said.

Caleb's fingers drummed against the railing. "Where's Mae?"

Then, on cue, the lightning outside flashed, and there was Mae. She stood on the other side of the foyer with her police-issued Glock handgun pointed at the intruder on the floor. "Freeze!" she shouted. "You're under arrest!"

My heart leaped—in a good way, for once. I'd almost been convinced that I was crazy, and Mae really was a hallucination induced by bumping my head in the basement. I nudged Craig. "Are you seeing this?"

"She's here, finally," he said.

I breathed a sigh of relief.

"Mae. Girl, your timing could not have been better," Marcus said as he eased his weight off the intruder. The man twitched as if he was going to make a run for it, but Mae's gun in his face convinced him to sit still. Marcus let him go and collapsed backward, gripping his side.

"Mae," I shouted down. There was no point in

being quiet anymore. "The other one is locked in the basement. He's injured."

"Ten-four. Well done. Thank you, Amy, for everything you have done for the family."

I realized I could hear her. The rain and thunder had stopped battering the house, and only the sound of trickling water surrounded us. Craig's arm around me squeezed, and it was so comforting that I almost leaned into him further.

On my other side, Caleb's grip on the railing was tight, his knuckles white. His eyes were focused wrong, as if he were seeing something beyond the walls of the foyer instead of the spectacle below. His lips twitched like he was rehearsing a speech.

Marcus kept a gun trained on the intruder while Mae reached into a belt full of tools strapped around her waist, out of place with the dress she was wearing, grey in the dim light of candles in other rooms. As Marcus chatted with his old friend, he seemed to grow confused.

"But how'd you get here so quickly?" I heard him ask.

Caleb was somewhere else. His face twitched into odd, momentary expressions. Something was still wrong here. I inhaled to suggest we go down to help deal with the men, but I was cut off by a gunshot.

Marcus collapsed. Mae was suddenly facing away from the intruder on the ground. Another crack echoed across the foyer, and her head snapped back.

Another man stepped across the foyer. He wore socks, making his footsteps nearly silent. His gas mask had two filters instead of one, forking in the middle, and his biohazard suit was old, cracking and peeling into tiny pieces in some areas. If the man in the basement was a pig, and the one on the floor a bear, then this new one was a snake.

Of course there were three of them. How could I have been so stupid? Three bears, three little pigs, three guesses to solve the riddle.

I withheld a scream. Marcus wasn't moving. Mae wasn't moving. The bear rose tall and collected each of their guns.

Caleb's eyes rolled back in his head. He convulsed against the railing as if it were electrified.

The power flashed again. This time the lights stayed on, illuminating the room below, illuminating us. We had to run, but before we did, I took one last glance down.

Mae's hat was beside her, in a spreading pool of blood, with a red rose on top. And her dress was bright orange.

PART IV
A SOLUTION

CHAPTER 10

I felt safe in the control room. Even though the intruders were still downstairs, dragging the bodies of people I'd likely have considered friends if I'd spent a bit more time with them, I felt safe. I felt guilty for feeling safe.

I'd be okay as long as I could see them. The power was back on, the cameras covered the main areas of the house, and the lock to the control room was solid, so I felt like I had at least some, well, control.

That didn't help the others. Behind me, as I monitored the house via the cameras, they each broke down in their own way.

I squeezed the mouse like it was the only thing keeping me from floating away. If I let go, my sanity would fly away as a fine mist and provide nutrients for the horrible trees outside.

Disconnected snippets of conversation reached my consciousness:

They're still out there!

What do they want?

Daddy!

But they're still out there!

What about Trista?

No, no, Daddy. My daddy.

They're still out there!

Where the heck is Ash?

Jasmine had been hiding in the control room, so Ash was the only member of the household still unaccounted for. I tried clicking to switch the cameras to other views to search for him, but the controls were still locked—hacked by whoever had planned this. Whoever had killed Trista.

One of those cameras still pointed at her. Nothing had changed. She was still dead. Her final message was still scrawled beside her, still too pixelated to read. Craig avoided looking at her, instead studying books on the shelves of the office as if getting to know a stranger's home, even though he'd probably put them there himself, and possibly even read them.

The intruders moved toward the edge of the camera's range. One of them appeared to be struggling as he dragged Marcus.

"Daddy!" Jasmine said, reaching out, her fingertip leaving a faint smudge on the screen.

The others—The Pig and The Snake, as I thought of

them—rushed to help The Bear move Marcus. They'd released The Pig from the basement, and it gave me a dark pleasure to see him limp into frame, and now struggle to help move Marcus with only one good hand.

A collection of dark-coloured pixels thrashed up and down on the screen. It was only a blur, but it very well could have been Marcus's boot, resisting these people once again. I hoped that's what it was. Jasmine sobbed and caressed the edges of the screen, clearly thinking the same thing, but nobody said anything, perhaps afraid of jinxing it. Hope was a rare and dangerous thing in this environment.

They moved off-camera for a few moments, then The Snake returned to the foyer. He looked around, shouting back to the others, his muffled voice audible through the door of the control room. The Pig entered the frame, scratching his head. He circled the room, his head swiveling back and forth. He checked behind a fake potted fern.

Mae's body was gone.

The family consoled each other around me. They didn't mention anything about Mae, so perhaps they were too distracted to notice. I tidied up my ponytail as my mind began working again. It was good they didn't notice. It was good that the body was gone, with not even a trace of blood, as if Mae had never been there at all. It was an odd event in a night of many, but at least this was one I had been half-expecting. Like all those confused scientists trying to figure out the environmental catastrophe, I had *theories* about what was occurring at Foster Manor.

The intruders moved off-camera again, toward the ball room.

I felt safer for a moment, even though I knew my sense of safety was false and temporary. These intruders hadn't killed Trista, after all. They didn't seem sophisticated enough, nor did they have the access necessary, to hack the security system. Someone from the Foster household had done that, though whether the murder was connected to the men down-stairs or the corrupted universe was playing loose with horrible coincidences, I did not know.

I put my ear up against the door. There were voices out there, but they were still distant, and I couldn't decipher anything they said. As far as I knew, the only way to get to us upstairs was to go through the foyer first, so we'd have advance warning on the cameras if—when—they came for us.

I nudged Caleb. He still acted strangely, staring at the walls of the small room like there was something written on them—transfixed by something just outside the range of vision the rest of us possessed. "Caleb, can you watch this camera?" I asked, pointing to the foyer view. Distraction would do us all some good. He slowly turned his head toward the computer screen, as if removing his gaze from the walls took physical effort. "If you see anyone, you need to say something."

He leaned forward, suddenly more alert. "I see someone."

It was Ash. He moved slowly, hunched over, tiptoeing as he stepped past the bottom of the staircase. "He's heading straight for those men, the intruders," I said. "We have to do something."

"What can we do?" Craig asked, after clearing his throat. He was too loud and frail to do much of anything.

"Some of us should go warn him," I said.

Jasmine shook her head. "I won't."

"He's one of us. We can't let him walk in there." Ash was making his way further down the hall. Soon he'd give himself away.

Jasmine shook her head again, the tears zigzagging down her face. Caleb only stared at the screen until his far-off glassy-eyed look returned and he was looking past it. I thought about Mae's speech about Jack again.

"I'll go. But you two need to come with me." I held up a hand when Jasmine and Caleb opened their mouths to protest. "We *need* to help him. If we don't, we'll regret it for the rest of our lives. Trust me."

They must have realized how certain I was in this fact from the mist forming in my eyes as I thought of Todd and Wes. Both of them stood taller, silently telling me they were, reluctantly, ready to go.

"Craig can watch the screen and shout a warning—only if absolutely necessary. Okay?"

As soon as Craig gave the slightest nod, I unlocked

the door, swung it open, and walked toward the stairs. Maybe I should have been more like this with my family—less turning away, more leading the way. It appeared to be working, because Jasmine and Caleb followed behind me.

Then I realized that my knee felt even puffier than before. I could barely walk, and right now the stairs looked like an obstacle course to me. But I faked it, squeezing the railing and easing myself down, one step at a time, realizing that each passing moment was another chance for Ash to get himself killed.

Who cares if he does?

I pushed the thought aside. From what little I knew of Ash, he was an asshole, but he was *the family's* asshole, and I wouldn't let another household disintegrate because of a few personality flaws and self-destructive tendencies. Jasmine and Caleb would realize that, too, if given the chance.

They rushed to help me down, trying to remain quiet, but my hand made squeaking noises on the polished wooden railing.

At the bottom of the stairs, I gestured toward the end of the hallway, where Ash approached the slight bend in the hall, leading to the rooms beyond, and the ball room at the end of the east wing where the intruders had gone. Jasmine and Caleb waved to try getting his attention, but he was oblivious. They creeped closer to him, making louder and louder *pssst!* noises.

That was my chance. Leading the way had its purpose, but turning away was what I did best.

I took a few steps back, then swiveled toward the west wing, and limped as quickly and quietly as I could to the basement, where Trista waited with a solution to all of this.

ﾞ

I hobbled down the hallway, away from the safety of the camera watching over me, away from the family. The power flashed in and out. Sconces on the walls got confused and flickered as they were fed an irregular flow of electricity. Thunder still roared outside, but it was distant now.

I almost reached the basement, but then a wave of nausea came over me, and suddenly it felt like the hallway was tipping over sideways. My knee was too weak to resist it, and I had to ease myself to the ground, clawing at the wainscoting.

I stared at the worn hardwood floor, making sure it was level with the rest of the Earth. It was. Of course it was. *It's only panic. Get yourself together, nerd.*

Strands of hair that had fallen loose from my ponytail blew to the side, tickling my ear. Something breathed heavily just behind me. The same hushed, scratchy voice that I'd heard hours ago, just after I arrived here.

What if, what if, what if.

I squeezed my eyes shut and told myself it was only the heating system again, making even odder sounds now because of the flickering power.

Louder now: *what if, what if.*

It wasn't the vents. I could feel the dampness of an open mouth behind my ear. Feel the heat of something large hovering there.

WHAT IF, WHAT IF, WHAT IF.

It sounded like screaming without vocal chords, just pure breath, a shouted whisper.

I swiveled and felt the heat behind me retreat. The lights went out just then, and the hall was black to my unadjusted eyes. But something moved down there. Something darker than the dark.

The power surged for a moment, the lights flickered, and there it was: the dog.

It was bigger than before, its shoulders almost as high as the sconces on the walls, occupying the bulk of hallway. Its fur was black with a few grey hairs, and slick with wetness.

I forced myself to turn and face it, then clutched at the intricate woodwork of the wall to pull myself up despite the protests of my knee.

It wasn't the heating system, but that didn't mean it was anything to be afraid of. "You're not real," I whispered.

I took a step toward it. It reared back and shook, sending droplets against the wall. The fur at the back of its neck stood on end and a low growl formed in its throat. I took another step forward.

"It's okay," I said in a voice as soothing as I could make it. "Maybe you don't even know you're doing this, but it's okay." I reached out, palm up and fingers curled, the way Wes had once taught me to approach a stranger's dog when we first walked along the ravine behind our new house. His ghost helping me out with this one. "We have a mutual friend, you and I. Mae? You know Mae, don't you, boy?"

The dog extended his neck toward my hand, yellow teeth underneath smacking lips.

It twitched toward my fingers.

I uncurled my hand and scratched underneath its chin. The fur and whiskers felt so real, just like I would have imagined them. Anyone who's ever had a dog could imagine the feeling of whiskers flowing around kneading fingertips.

"You're imaginary, aren't you, boy?" I whispered, trying to project calm even as I noticed red coming off on my hand where I'd stroked the dog's damp fur. Blood dripped down the walls from when he'd shaken the wetness off. "Just like Mae."

He wagged his tail at the mention of her name. I giggled and stroked the side of his neck, making him flop onto his side, the ground thumping beneath him. As I scratched his belly, his long black legs, the size of a deer's, flailed in the air. I had to move my face back to avoid getting scratched by overgrown black claws.

Keep moving, urged my inner voice of reason.

When I stopped rubbing the dog's belly, he twisted upright and looked at me with big, sad eyes, a high-pitched whine in his throat.

"It's okay, boy. Go find Mae! She'll play with you."

Sure enough, she was behind him now, standing further down the hall, alive and well. I walked toward her, and the dog followed, his big tongue flopping out as he ran ahead and approached Mae, claws clacking on the hardwood.

What colour was her hat? The sconces flicked on and it was green. They flicked off, then on again, and now it was orange.

She crouched to pat the dog. As he licked her face, she looked up at me with her kind, grandmotherly smile, and I tried to smile back. She turned and headed toward the foyer, like a normal old woman taking her normal blood-soaked dog for a walk.

Suddenly I remembered the camera perched outside, above the entryway. Would Craig spot them leaving? My face turned hot. The nagging feeling that I was going crazy came on again, but they'd *all* seen Mae's attempt to rescue us. She wasn't my imagination —I'd asked Craig. *She's here, finally,* he'd said. But what if his insistence that she wasn't imaginary was part of my imagination too?

Or: what if the ghosts were imaginary, but not part of *my* imagination?

What if, what if, what if.

Murder. Murder was easier to figure out. Murder

was something that happened in the real world. Trista wasn't a ghost, not really, but maybe she could still tell me who killed her.

&

It was seeing Craig and Caleb's bond that had finally reminded me of the failsafe code. At first it was only a tickle at the back of my mind when Craig touched Caleb's chin to better examine him. I'd seen that same gesture before:

Todd fell off his tricycle—the little plastic one with a wooden handle that his dad could push and steer from behind, so it was pretty much idiot proof. Somehow, Todd fell off anyway, spilling onto the grass beside the sidewalk. Wes crouched beside him, then did that exact same gesture, pushing Todd's head from side to side to make sure he was okay. I watched it all from the porch, worried at first, but then relieved that Todd was okay, and that his dad was there to watch over him. *Perhaps this start to our new life together in this new home won't be so bad after all,* I'd thought, at the time.

The next day, getting started in the marketing department at APT, I needed a password. The glow of Todd and Wes still in my mind, it came to me easily:

Eden0306

It was the name of the street our little new house was on, Eden Place, and the dates of Todd's and Wes's birthdays.

I had to change my passwords over the years, of course, but the four-digit code came back as the failsafe code to verify my entry into debugging mode on all of APT's security systems.

I entered the key combo to enter debug mode on the panel outside the safe room, then the failsafe code: 0 3 0 6. I wouldn't need Gary's strings-attached help. I wouldn't even need electricity. All I needed was my family, dead but not gone.

Ghosts, but not really.

Trista was in a similar state. The door to her final resting place unlocked with a clink, and the handle, roughened thanks to Caleb chiseling away at it, felt cold in my hand.

I thought of Trista's diary. She'd mentioned the man—*HE*—watching her, smelling of cherries. And another person, *SHE*, was equally terrifying to her. Two prime suspects in her death. She'd had one final word to write, and it was scrawled in her own blood beside her, inside that room. It must be the name of her killer. That had to be it; what else would a life-long diary writer do in her final moments? The answer was just behind the door. So why was I hesitating?

I pushed through. My family's ghostly shadow had gotten me here. Trista's would get me through the next step. The door swung open. The fresh, cool, filtered air blew loose strands of hair back from my forehead.

When I saw what was inside, my heart felt like it

was pumping sludge. My knee gave out. I had to lean against the door frame to stay upright.

Trista didn't have answers about who killed her.

The room didn't have answers either. The room was a liar. It had promised me a solution. Now it only gave me the impossible.

This place didn't make sense. This *universe* didn't make sense. Someone had built this house, this shelter, in the middle of a forest, where trees and wild animals were forged through the chaotic laws of nature, following programming in their DNA designed to harvest energy, then protect it.

I'd built this shelter within the shelter. Programmed for the same purpose—preserving energy, preserving life. It failed, like everything would. Something bigger always wants that energy. Life splays out. Meat never stays on the carcass. The universe always tends toward entropy.

I wanted to scream, but why? Why waste the energy? Laughing would be more appropriate, but equally futile.

I took a step back, away from the horror inside the safe room. My back hit something that wasn't there before.

A hand clamped around my mouth. Tobacco and sweat filled my nose. Flaking nylon scratched against my elbows as I thrashed, but The Snake was strong, and like an actual python, squeezed harder the more I struggled. The back of my head smashed against the double-mouthpiece of his gas mask, in the tender spot I'd already hit against the stone floor last time I was in the basement, placing me back in that state of grogginess. My useless knee made it easy for him to drag me from the safe room, where more hands grabbed me from every angle.

Then I felt something I didn't expect to feel, getting away from that horrible safe room, probably for the last time: relief.

CHAPTER 11

The ball room's carpet smelled like a dog. Probably the same dog Craig had played with here when he was younger, and I imagined as shaggy and black, like the one Mae had taken out to play. The Foster family dog was long dead, but I could smell it, and unlike the spectral dog that had stalked me since I arrived, the smell was *real*. I could *feel* it in my nose, in a way I couldn't feel the home's dreamlike apparitions.

I had time to contemplate this as one man held me against the carpet so hard that the fibres tickled my nostrils, while another one rifled through a bag for a zip tie. One of them—The Snake, I think—finally looped the plastic tie around my wrists behind me. My arms shook with effort as he clicked it tight.

They hauled me onto a dining chair draped in white linen, then tied my ankles together too. Outside, the storm picked up again, the strange red glow of the lightning-infused sky casting shadows of trees against the ball room's many tall windows.

Craig sat beside me, then Jasmine, Caleb, Ash, and Marcus—all tied up and lined up in the order we were captured. Marcus's chest rose and fell—he was alive, but his face was ashen. A blossom of blood soaked the chair covering, turning the fabric red almost all the way to the floor. The Bear yanked Marcus's head back and looked into his eyes, which were open, but didn't seem to register anything.

The Bear mumbled something to The Snake, then the three men stomped to the other side of the room to talk in whispers.

"I'm sorry," Craig said.

Caleb whimpered words that didn't sound English, but his father's apology silenced him. "Sorry for what, Dad?"

"When you didn't come back upstairs, I had to come down to find you. I was supposed to save you. I'm supposed to be the dad here." His last few words tumbled out along with a cough.

"It's not your fault, Dad. None of this is your fault."

Jasmine sniffed back tears. "Yeah, fuck off with that apology, Craig."

Marcus looked up, suddenly lucid for a moment. "She's right, Craig, buzz off with the blame. You're making us dads look bad. Besides, I'm the one that went and got myself shot," he growled.

Then, somehow, we all laughed. Everyone except Ash.

But whose fault was it really? Because I knew now that someone here was to blame. Someone here had killed Trista with *HIS* or *HER* own hands. And surely it wasn't coincidence that these men had shown up tonight, of all nights, so someone was to blame for that too.

"Someone did it," I mumbled while the others continued to chuckle through their tears. "Someone here is responsible."

They fell silent. Finally, Ash spoke. "Bet it was the cough that gave you away, got you captured, wasn't it, Craig?"

Craig's sigh sounded like it had sand in it. "What's your point, Ash?"

"Same point I've had all along. We all knew that cough would kill you, just not this soon. Caleb knew it better than anyone. He knew that he wouldn't get the inheritance when the day came—not with Trista ahead of him in the line."

"You take that back!" Caleb squealed.

One of the men behind us told us to shut up.

Caleb lowered his voice. "You know I wouldn't. You all know I wouldn't. Right? Right? Even Amy believes me."

"I know you didn't," Craig said. "I was with you in the family room just before. I headed upstairs to bed, and it was only a minute later when Jasmine saw ... her

… my baby … on the camera. There was no time. There's no way."

"Yeah, but can we ever trust what comes from your mouth, Craig?" Ash's face was red, his usual sarcastic detachment gone. "I couldn't even trust you to pay me on time."

"This again? Now?" Craig said.

"Listen. You couldn't pay me on time, even though you could damn well afford it. Just like you could damn well afford Trista's tuition." Ash paused to let Craig say something, but he didn't. "Look at his face, everyone. That guilt! My god, it's like a puppy caught destroying the baby's favourite stuffy. Yeah, so, I heard your little conversation with Trista. More of a fight than a conversation, really. That was just before she left for a week, touring the universities she was hell-bent on running away to, and you refused to pay for. 'I wish I could just lock you in the safe room forever'—a direct quote."

Craig's face twisted with confusion, and, yes, some guilt. "It … it was a joke. Of course it was. How did you kn—"

"I hear things. I always hear things. I'm always here. I haunt this place like it's my job, because it's where I'm, sometimes, paid to be. No, I wouldn't leave you, poor fragile lonely Craig, not like Trista. And Jasmine, weren't you—" Ash said.

"Ash, now it's your turn to fuck off," Marcus said.

"Says the man who can't accept his own daughter. Can't accept who she is. What she is."

160

"Just what do you think you know about *what* I am, Ash?" Jasmine screamed through a veil of tears.

"Shut up! Shut *up!*" shouted The Bear.

We shut up. In the ensuing silence, I heard fragments of what the intruders said to each other. "If it's not here tonight, it's coming any day now," one of them said.

"Are we even sure the room's really safe?" another said, later.

More frantic whispering.

Another raised his voice. "Cost? *Cost?*"

A moment later: "He's right, I'd rather be alive and feeling guilty than dead and feeling nothing."

They were talking about killing us. They were talking about the mental toll of killing us. We didn't have any time left.

Out of necessity, a plan that had been percolating through my mind finally reached my lips and trickled out. "Listen. I heard Craig coughing just before Jasmine's scream, when Trista was killed. That was when he headed upstairs, just like he said. It couldn't have been him. He was with Caleb moments earlier, so it wasn't Caleb. Caleb said that Marcus was cleaning up in the kitchen, and I heard the pipes rattling, so it wasn't Marcus. Mae didn't get here until later. Jasmine was in the control room at the time, and Jasmine, didn't you say you stepped out to talk to Ash just as it happened?"

Jasmine simmered with rage when she looked at Ash, but she nodded her head.

"So it wasn't Jasmine, it wasn't Ash."

"That's everyone," Caleb said. "I told you!"

"You were right." I was convincing Caleb, which was exactly what I needed. It was what we all needed, even though everything I said was irrelevant at best, fiction at worst. But wasn't Mae fiction? Weren't the legends of Jack just stories?

I brought the fiction home—tacked on the powerful ending, the emotional gut punch. "We've eliminated everyone who lives here. That only leaves them."

"But the security syst—" Craig said.

"It's not foolproof, okay?" Here was the part where the storyteller's faults helped drive the message home. "There are vulnerabilities. We don't tell customers that, of course, but nothing is impenetrable. With the right information, the right codes, anything can be hacked. And these men, they must have hacked it. While we were sitting and eating in the family room, or maybe even well before that, these men disabled the security system, slipped in through the back door, into the basement, and murdered Trista. The safe room wasn't safe. The home wasn't safe. It never was."

Ash regarded me with a mix of bafflement and out-of-place amusement. Caleb began to tremble. That was good. I leaned forward in my chair so he could see my face.

"Maybe the plan was to put all of you in the safe

room, not just Trista. While they robbed the house. But Trista came home from her university tour earlier than planned and caught them here, so they locked her up. These men saw the risk of Trista giving away that they were out there in the woods, waiting. There are pens and paper in the safe room; a note pointed toward the camera would ruin their plans the moment Ash checked the security system." I glanced at the men. They were too caught up in their own argument to notice me talking, but I tried to keep my voice down nonetheless. "So they killed her," I whispered. "They walked into that room and they bludgeoned her with a hammer. It looks like the first few blows didn't do it, so they had to keep going at her while she crawled toward the yellow door and begged for her life."

None of this was true.

Jasmine weeped. Caleb had his far-off look again, like he was looking past me, out into the woods, where the trees thrashed about like madmen in an asylum.

"How do you know? How did you get into the room?" Craig asked.

"Same way they did," I said, trying to direct the conversation to address Caleb, but Craig was getting agitated and red-faced between us. "You thought you were safe, and that was a mistake. It was stupid. These men took advantage of that. They're like all the other scared men out there—they'll do anything to feel safe, even if it means giving in to chaos. To death."

"Are you saying this is my f-f-" Craig began, but was

interrupted by his coughing. Flecks of red appeared on his khaki pants as he hacked.

"Shut up!" one of the men shouted.

My heart was breaking. "No, no, it's not your fault. You just wanted to protect your family. *They* took advantage of that."

Caleb's head slowly turned as he took his attention away from the forest outside and onto the men. His expression became blank, his focus soft, as if he were daydreaming about a memory from the distant past.

Craig coughed as tears streamed down his face. I reached my aching, restrained arms toward him and managed to wrap my right pinkie finger around his left. "I'm so sorry," I said.

His stare met mine as he nodded. His pinkie squeezed mine. Red dots appeared on the front of his shirt as he failed to contain the ragged cough.

"I said shut up!" The Bear stomped over to stand in front of Craig. The Snake followed behind, little flecks falling from his peeling hazard suit and leaving a sparkling trail in his wake. I could feel The Pig's eyes on me as he hovered behind us.

The Bear glanced at The Snake, then pointed at Craig. "Kill him."

Jasmine screamed.

The Snake raised his gun, but his hand shook violently. "We can find another way."

"That's not the plan. It's *our turn.* That's the plan.

The weak have lived comfortable lives, but the world has now provided a gift for the strong."

The Snake took a step forward, the gun an inch from Craig's forehead. This wasn't part of the plan, but there was nothing I could do. Any movement and I'd be dead first. I could feel The Pig's ragged breath tickling the back of my neck.

"We can let them run. Look at that storm," The Snake said, gesturing with the gun to the trees outside the window, whipping back and forth in the storm's second wind. "Time's up. They won't come back. They can't identify us."

The Bear ripped his gas mask off. He couldn't have been older than thirty, and had light hair, grey eyes, a face I would have described as soft, kind. He could've been anybody. He could've been Wes. "They can identify us now, Alex. You are Alex James, and your five-year-old son Aiden is waiting at your former home on Castor Crescent. Do it for Aiden, Alex. Do it for his future."

The Snake—Alex—pulled the trigger.

Craig fell silent. His finger slipped away from mine. His head slumped forward. The trickle of blood from his face matched the trickle of the reddened rain running past the windows.

Jasmine screamed. The Bear pointed at her, then at The Pig. "Charlie. Your turn."

"Guys, come on," Ash said, breaking his unusual streak of silence.

Marcus had sagged to one side, unconscious. Maybe dead.

"They did this," I whispered to Caleb, my voice so wracked with emotion that it did not sound anything like me. "Your sister. Marcus. Now your father."

Caleb's eyes rolled back in his head. His lips moved, reciting fragments of sentences that made no sense together, various names of animals and people spilling from his mouth in rapid succession.

"Charlie!" bellowed The Bear. His face was no longer kind. The Pig—Charlie—put the tip of his handgun against the back of Jasmine's head. His arm dipped for a moment, and I thought he may have been losing consciousness from all the holes I'd put in him, but then he raised the gun again and put it against my head instead.

"Her first," he said.

A rumble filled the house, stopped, then started again. It sounded like a large truck was rolling toward the house, or—no, more like something massive was *stepping* towards the house.

"Jasmine! Ash! Close your eyes!" I shouted. The tip of The Pig's gun pulled out some of my hair as he suddenly swiveled toward the window and squealed.

The Bear and The Snake began to turn. I squeezed my eyes shut.

"What is that?" The Snake asked.

Behind me, The Pig crashed against a cart holding dishes and silverware as he launched himself away from the window. He laughed nervously. "No," he said. "No no no, I'm the wolf. *I'm* the wolf."

The ground rumbled again. Or did it only feel like it was rumbling because of my shaking legs? Was I doing this to myself, like in those old TV shows where the actors threw themselves around to simulate a crumbling starship?

"What's going on?" Jasmine cried.

"Are your eyes shut?" I asked.

"Yes."

"Keep them shut. All of you, keep your eyes shut!"

But Ash made a very strange sound, exhaling with his nose repeatedly like an agitated horse. His eyes weren't closed.

A thump to my left let me know that The Snake had fallen over. His flaky hazard suit scratched against the carpet as he writhed on the ground.

"Fee fi, fee fi, fee fi," Caleb mumbled.

All at once, thunder crashed, and one of the windows shattered. The room filled with humid wind laced with that sickly-sweet smell of the environmental catastrophe.

"It's them!" screamed The Bear. He fired his gun at the front of the house. "We can't hide from *that*. Hah! We were so stupid, we could never hide. It's their turn. Run!"

He fired again. Something moaned, so deep and powerful that my chair buzzed, the silverware and wall hangings rattled. It was like a mountain exhaling.

Whose story was this? Caleb was the creator. His anger and his own stories were manifesting here at Foster Manor, as I knew they would, as they always had. But the men had their own experience of the story, their own interpretation.

I could hear crackling around me. I was convinced the walls were on fire. I felt radiating warmth on my face.

The Snake got free from whatever he'd been struggling with. "Aiden! Is that you? How did you get out there? Get away from the window! Charlie, where are the keys? We need to get him out of here."

But The Pig had bolted; he ran past me, leaving a gust of air in his wake. A moment later, another gust, lower to the ground, tickled my ankles.

The Bear laughed maniacally. "They're everywhere at once! How can you hide when they're everywhere at once? All we can do is run. All we can *do* is run!"

"Down, blow your house, huff 'n puff, huff 'n puff, down," Caleb muttered. I felt him convulsing in his chair.

Wind filled the room. Leaves and branches scraped at my face and my lungs burned from the acrid air. A drop of water hit me in the eyebrow and I instinctively twitched to get rid of it, and without thinking, opened one eye.

Dark shapes were all around. The sun had started to rise, but something blocked it, keeping the room and the laneway out front dark. A smaller shadow skittered closer to the ground outside on the laneway, where The Pig fell to the ground, screaming, before the shadow overtook him.

Flames licked at the walls, but I knew that wasn't real. I knew that was just me.

The Bear stumbled just before reaching the window, the gust of wind too strong. The gun fell from his hands. He pinwheeled backward, toward Marcus. Then he regained his footing and stepped forward again.

A loud snap came from Marcus. He'd found the strength to break the zip ties holding his arms, which were soon wrapped around The Bear's neck. Marcus's shoes flew off as he kicked to break the legs off the chair and escape the ties around his feet. As The Bear tried to escape, they both toppled forward, through the remaining shards of the broken window, glass slashing at them both.

I squeezed my eyes shut before I could see more. I wished I could close my ears against the warbling wail from outside. Was it only the wind? Or was Marcus somehow making that inhuman sound?

The Snake shouted for his son. "Come back, Aiden! Where are you going?" His voice got further and further away.

Tears streamed down my face. I thought about Todd. What were the last things he heard as he burned? Did he die with his eyes open or his eyes closed?

I concentrated on what his face looked like. I held that in my mind's eye to block out the sounds and feelings around me—the screams, the thumps, the wind, the heat, the rumbling of the Earth.

I don't know how long it was before I allowed the world back in, and there was finally silence.

When I opened my eyes, Jasmine and I were the only conscious beings around. Caleb had passed out. Ash was gone.

CHAPTER 12

My wrists ached. The trick to escaping zip ties is to keep your fists clenched tight and palms facing down as your captors put them on—it hurts, but it creates more room between your wrists. You keep your arms flexed in this uncomfortable position no matter how tight they squeeze, struggling right from the start so you don't have to struggle later.

That didn't always work out so neatly when it came to other parts of my life. Here, it was struggle all the way down.

As if sensing my pain, Jasmine briefly squeezed my arm.

At least the sun felt good on my face. The rain had finally stopped beating down, and the house seemed oddly peaceful in the morning light spilling through the shattered windows.

"It's over," Jasmine said. She couldn't take her eyes off the unmoving lumps outside. One of them could have been her father, but she was in no rush to confirm that. I could already tell that he was gone, in the same way I could tell that Caleb's assault was done—the rumble and buzz from just a few minutes earlier was absent, though my ears still rang.

"It's not over," I whispered. "I have to show you something."

We untied Caleb, laid him on the ground, and put a bunched-up table cloth under his head. A trickle of blood fell from his nose as his eyes gradually opened.

"You did it," I said. "They're gone, Caleb. The house is ours."

"Our turn." He smiled, but he wasn't happy.

I brushed a curl of hair back from his face and fought back tears. "We'll get you out of here soon. Just rest for a minute."

He shook his head and glanced at his father, still slumped in his chair. "I'll stay. I'll protect Dad. And Trista. Get help and I'll stay."

I nodded and wiped snot from my nose. "Okay, honey." That's what I'd called Todd, but only when he was very young. "We'll get help."

I handed him The Snake's discarded pistol, in case any of them came back, even though the gun seemed tiny and ineffectual in his hands now. He had power greater than any gun. I didn't know how it worked, but he'd summoned something that protected us all.

172

Perhaps it was only imagination he summoned, provoking something already inside the people around him, but it had done the job. The unmoving lumps outside could attest to that.

I grabbed the rifle The Pig had abandoned, then took Jasmine to the safe room. She hesitated at the top of the stairs to the basement. "I don't need to see her."

"Sorry, but you do. You'd never believe me if I told you."

"You already did. Trista is in there, bludgeoned to death with a hammer by those men. I already know too much." She shook and whimpered as she exhaled. "I'll already see that every time I close my eyes for the rest of my life. I love her so much, Amy. Dad didn't like it—he's traditional like that—and Craig didn't like it much either, because of how much she loved me. We were going to run away together. Just a few more months here, then we'd have been off to university together, past all this jealousy, away from this place. Those men ruined it. I'm guilty too, though."

I tensed. "Why would you feel guilty?"

Tears sparkled on her cheeks in the rising sun. "She sent me a text message just before she came home, a few days ago. Her university trip was supposed to last all week, but she said she only needed to see one campus to make her decision. She started with a tour of Queens, but she knew that if she went there, it would be just like it was during the tour—without me. I'd already accepted my offer from Western University. She said that the beauty of the campus meant nothing to her without me." Jasmine sobbed. "I should have told her to keep going, make the right decision for her career, but I was selfish. When she said her mind was made up, and she'd be going to Western with me, I told her how happy that made me. Selfish! She came home right away. And if she hadn't, if she didn't love me like I love her, she'd have still been touring those universities alone when those men came for her."

I let her cry until she couldn't anymore, then waited a minute longer, but there was no right time to say it, so I just said it: "The men didn't do it. They didn't kill her."

"What?"

"I'll show you."

We descended into the basement once more. The power was back, but the lights only made it more horrible to step past the rubber castle, where small pools of blood were dry on the edges but still wet in the middle, resembling suckers on a rubbery tentacle. And had the door to the safe room always been such a sickly yellow? Or had I just never seen it so clearly before?

I tried the family's passcode again, just to test if having the power back would somehow reset it, but no dice—as I knew now, someone had intentionally changed every passcode. So I typed in the failsafe passcode of my dead family's birthdays, looked around to make sure nobody was following us, then opened the door.

Jasmine recoiled from what she saw, just as I had. Trista was there. She was dead. But she hadn't been killed last night.

Trista almost appeared peaceful on the bed. Jasmine covered her nose and stepped inside. "No. Someone moved her? But …"

I let her draw more conclusions on her own. Trista's skin was blotchy and had a sheen to it. She was a slim girl in the photos I'd seen on the Fosters' fridge, but now her belly had bloated so much that it stretched the buttons of her flannel shirt. It was marked by a single stab wound on the left side.

"But where did …" Jasmine stammered, looking at the clean white floor. There was no blood, and no message scrawled in it. Trista's final message was gone. Long gone.

I checked behind us again to make sure we were alone.

"He cleaned it up," I said. "He had a few days to do it."

"No. No, I saw her, just last night. She was fine until I stepped out, and then she … wasn't. That was last night."

"You only saw her last night on the cameras."

"But that's the camera right there," she said, pointing to the black hemisphere in the ceiling.

"They're live when it's working. When the whole system hasn't been hacked. He rewound the security tape to hide what he did. I don't know if he meant for us to see her dead, or if he thought we'd all be gone by the time the tape got to that point. He knew when that point was; I saw him checking his watch all the time, though I didn't know why. At the exact time when the tape got to her killing, that's when he distracted you, to make sure you didn't see him. But if you did, you'd be seeing into the past. She was killed three days ago."

"Ash. Of course." She shivered. "He's been with us all night, hiding this. But why? Why would he do this? Where is he now?"

I thought of Trista's diary—the *HE* who smelled like cherries and stood outside her room at night. "More jealousy? Did he love her?"

Love was powerful. Didn't Trista's diary say that *SHE*—Jasmine—was just as frightening as Ash?

Jasmine shook her head, then kneeled beside Trista and took her pale hand. "He's about the only one who didn't actually love her. Oh he'd *say* he loved her, if you pressed him. Maybe he even believed it. But he didn't love her. He just *wanted* her. She was an object to him—I could see it in the way he looked her up and down when she walked into a room. She defended him, said he was practically a part of the family, but when I suggested we move away, far away, she didn't protest, and I think getting away from him was part of why she didn't even consider staying here."

I put it together, but there were still missing pieces. It couldn't have been a coincidence that the intruders came to the house tonight, just after Ash had done his business with Trista. I speculated out loud about what could have happened—Ash had planned on giving the house, with its safe room, to the intruders. They were some of the growing number of cultish true believers fearing the end of the world, desperate for somewhere safe, so they could have promised Ash anything in return. Money, their old homes, maybe even a spot in the safe room.

HE is planning something, her diary, her ghost, had said.

"She must have caught him planning this. She went to investigate what he was up to, in the safe room, and he locked her in there. He went back to talk her out of revealing what he'd been planning—or do something even worse to her—and she wouldn't."

"Of course she wouldn't. She was so strong," Jasmine said, squeezing Trista's cold hand.

"So he killed her. He got scared, ran off, but then came back later to clean up. Maybe he was planning on hiding her body, too, but Craig and Caleb came back home from their vacation before he could. The attackers were watching the house, and all the activity accelerated their plans to move in. They tried to scare us out, with the writing on the window, but when that didn't work, they took a more direct approach."

Jasmine stood. She leaned forward and kissed Trista on the forehead. Then she seemed to become aware of where she was, glancing at the space behind me. "So where is Ash?"

I squeezed the rifle. "They probably never even tied him up properly in the ball room. Let's hope he ran away and isn't planning on coming back. I'm not sure how much he saw. If he opened his eyes, his mind might be mush, just like those men."

"It was Caleb, wasn't it? We've always seen things when he's around. When he's emotional, it gets worse. None of us said it out loud, because that's crazy, but it was him, wasn't it? He made them see things. He saved us."

"I think so."

"And *you* provoked him. You lied about what you saw down here. You barely know us; how did you know what would happen?"

I turned away. "I didn't know for sure. But I tested him, before that. I told him Mae was wearing an orange hat. It wasn't orange—it was green, I'm sure it was— but when Mae appeared again, well, you saw it."

Jasmine gasped. "Mae was never really here."

"No," I said. My bottom lip trembled as I thought about it all—Mae, the dog, the flying glass in the séance. Would I be able to go home and live life as if the world made sense? As if anything were really *real?*

We embraced, then, and cried for a long while, letting all the hurt and confusion release itself, until we were, at least temporarily, able to function again.

My phone still didn't function, however, so we'd need to get out of here to find help. I locked the safe room, then, upstairs, reset the system so only Jasmine and I could alter any settings. The camera went back to the live view of Trista, terrible but true. Caleb would stay and guard the house from any more tampering. If it came to defending himself, he probably wouldn't even need the gun.

I felt like the house was secure again. I'd done my job. It wasn't a fairy-tale ending, but it would have to do.

They'd slashed my tires. I gained a small comfort in knowing that if I'd tried to abandon the family and drive away, as my natural inclinations would have led me to do, it probably would have ended up with me dead. There was storybook justice in that.

But during Caleb's defence of the home, I'd heard something about keys. The Snake had yelled at The Pig for keys, presumably the ones for the big white truck semi-hidden off the laneway, blocked by trees enough that it would have been invisible in the dark, but in the morning light it stood out against the natural backdrop like a rotting thumb.

The Pig lay on the ground between the house and the truck. His mask had been torn off and tossed beside him. Little rivers of red dried around the driveway's cobblestones, spreading like veins away from his faded pink hazard suit. The cartilage of his Adam's apple showed under the gouges criss-crossing his neck. I'd seen a shadow overtake him, but could Caleb's apparitions kill? Or were The Pig's red fingernails proof that he had done this to himself?

I heaved as I undid his suit to reach the pocket of his jeans and pull out a key. I clicked the unlock button and the truck's headlights flashed.

"Jasmine?" I shouted, turning toward the house.

She came out a moment later, gently closing the door behind her. She shook her head as her shoes clomped across the driveway. "Caleb won't come. I explained what happened with his sister. He said he's staying with his family, and staying with the house."

I understood. Even though the family would have seemed normal to anyone else, doing normal family things, I couldn't picture Caleb in particular outside of the house. When I tried to imagine the Fosters out at a restaurant, maybe celebrating Trista's birthday, there was a blank space where Caleb should have been. Instead, he was back at the house. Part of the house.

Jasmine let me use her shoulder to take some weight off my knee. She offered to drive, but I told her I'd be fine once I sat down.

I thought I heard a distant thumping. It could have

been a neighbour clearing brush, but my mind heard the beat of another song from Graceland, even filling in some of Paul Simon's lyrics. When we reached the truck, I turned back for one last look at the Foster Manor. It seemed to writhe with life, breathe with Caleb's breath, as it whispered Craig's music. Shadows moved in the windows, and if I squinted I could make out Mae's hat—green or orange, I couldn't tell—and a pair of canine eyes peeking over the windowsill. Despite all the death in that place, it buzzed of life.

Jasmine got in the passenger seat of the truck and drummed her fingers on the dashboard. I got the hint and pulled myself into the driver's side.

"Seatbelts," I said.

Jasmine rolled her eyes, in a way that Todd and Wes did sometimes when I was overly cautious with them.

"It seems ridiculous, doesn't it? A seatbelt, after all this. But you know, safety is what I do. For better or worse," I said, thinking of the safe room.

I got a sad smile out of Jasmine, and she did follow my lead to strap up.

We pulled away and drove through the forest, back to civilization. As the thump and buzz of life from the house faded, we kept an eye out for other signs of life—Ash, or Marcus. There was no sign of them in the forest, which was incongruously beautiful in the translucent mist from the previous night's storm, high-lighting shafts of light beaming from space to the Earth.

Jasmine slumped in her seat and wept quietly.

&.

Something was wrong, but I couldn't put my finger on what.

Relax, Amy, you're free, I told myself.

Perhaps it was the storm. They had never lasted so long before. I could see puffs of red clouds over the tops of the trees lining the country roads, which were a sign that the environmental catastrophe was not over, and was instead getting worse. Maybe the men who attacked the house for its safe room had the right idea. Maybe there were no rules when the end of the world was coming.

Don't be ridiculous, I thought, *there is still time. There is still beauty in the world worth preserving.*

Jasmine's puffy brown eyes drooped shut—her body needed sleep after being awake all night, despite the thoughts that must have been torturing her mind. There was beauty in that. There was beauty in the little smear of grease from where her forehead rested against the window. There was even beauty in the red clouds that had appeared in the world, threatening to end it, but adding a darkly sweet smell to the air.

I inhaled. That's what was wrong.

The truck smelled like cherries.

I checked the rearview mirror. The road behind me

was clear. But my gaze lingered on the back seat, and I thought I heard a scratch of fabric against fabric.

Jasmine sensed my tension and snapped to attention. I put my foot on the brake, swiped the turn signal, and began to pull over.

Ash—*HIM*—thrust up from the floor of the back seat. Suddenly he had an arm around Jasmine, and one of her father's kitchen knives to her throat.

"Keep driving!" he said. His wild eyes and shaky voice now lacked his trademark veneer of sarcastic detachment.

"You fuck!" Jasmine said, and attempted to turn around, but he leaned forward to rest on the wide center console of the truck and press the knife against her neck hard enough to draw blood.

Jasmine pressed herself back in her seat. "You've ruined me, Ash. You've ruined this whole family. My dad, Trista. I loved her so much."

"You think I didn't love her?" Ash said.

"You only wanted to fuck her. You wanted to use her. Just like you tried to let those men use their home."

The knife shook in his hand. "Don't you put this on me. They were only supposed to scare you all off. Write on the windows, let off a few warning shots. It was supposed to be gradual, but then ... that ... that storm moved up their plans. That haunted fucking house distracted you from the warning signs, like it wanted to keep you there even if it killed you. And fucking *Trista!*"

"Ash, don't you even say her name," Jasmine said.

"She read my text messages, you know that? The scrawny bitch snuck into my room while I was watering her orchids and cutting her lawn, and thought she could invade what little privacy I had left. If you ran off with her, you'd have seen her dark side too."

Jasmine shook with anger. "She trusted me. I didn't sneak around her room at night. I didn't stare at her like she was a slab of meat. Why did you kill her, Ash?"

He bared his teeth. "Because I didn't have time to keep her locked in that room until she starved."

Jasmine twitched with anger, and the knife came millimetres from carving into her neck.

I needed to do something. "Where are we going, Ash?"

He glanced at the open road ahead of us. His eyes were rimmed with red and twitched wildly, seeing things that we didn't; he definitely didn't keep them closed while the invaders lost their minds. He gave me an address. "You think one safe room would have held all of us? No, that was just for Alex and his kid. There are two more safe rooms that your company was kind enough to build for us. You saw what was out there, in the storm." He shook like he was freezing. "There's no time left. Those … those *things* are out there, and soon we'll all be their slaves. You saw them, didn't you?"

"No, Ash," I said.

"They'll enslave us all!" he said, his voice hysterical.

"Keep driving and get me to the next house, and you won't get hurt."

But he'd killed Trista for knowing less. The moment we dropped him off to terrorize a new family, we'd join the pile of bodies Ash had left behind him. That was a problem—an unacceptable security risk.

I shook my head. "Scared men," I said.

"What?"

"The end of the world is beating at our doorstep, and it's still scared men making things worse instead of better."

"What the fuck are you talking about?"

It was the first thing that came in my mind, and perhaps I was only stalling. I'd devoted my life to safety and security. It didn't always work—for the Foster family, the safe room had created more problems than it solved. But sometimes safety measures did the job they were designed to do.

Plus, I'd vowed to start tackling my problems head on.

I floored the gas pedal and turned the wheel sharply. The truck veered off the road and down an embankment. I aimed for the nearest tree.

When the bumper wrapped itself around the tree, the safety belts around Jasmine and me did their jobs, but Ash was not so lucky. As the front of the truck crumpled, he flew through the windshield, hit the tree, and came to resemble the red mist that he'd been so frightened of.

My life didn't flash before my eyes. I didn't see Todd and Wes waving up at me from the sky; no, my imagination was not as vivid as Caleb's, and certainly not as … external. But I did *think* of my family, and how many times in the past twelve hours I'd been close to joining them.

Judging by how Jasmine was staring at the red paste on the tree that used to be Ash, she was not seeing her family either—her girlfriend Trista, her father Marcus, both dead or likely to be. She was as much an orphan as me now.

"Are you hurt?" I asked.

"Why did you—where—" she stammered, in shock.

I helped her unlatch her seatbelt. Both front doors were buckled so badly that they wouldn't open, so we crawled into the back seat of the truck, past a worn-down tube of red lipstick, past a discarded wrapper for a cherry candy, and spilled out a back door onto the shoulder of the road.

When we'd crawled far enough away from the car to be sure it wouldn't hurt us if it exploded, the pain set in. My knee still wouldn't bend. My forehead felt slick from where it had left a layer of skin on the truck's airbag. Jasmine's breaths were shallow and shaky; perhaps from the shock, perhaps from a few broken ribs.

I took her hand in mine. It calmed her down, and

gave her a job to do, because I could barely support my weight without her steadying me after every step.

We'd crashed in front of a driveway. We limped up a dirt road until we could see past the trees, to where the driveway was leading, hoping that it would be somewhere with a phone, or there would be someone there who could help us.

It was a house. A mix of old and new, it had a central foyer, with wings stretching to either side. The bulge at the end of the west wing could have been a ball room. A few APT Security signs poked out of the front garden like hexagonal flowers.

Jasmine and I looked at each other.

"No," she said.

"Not in a million years."

So we continued walking, slowly. We were sad, we were in pain, the sky darkened above us, but we continued walking, and we imagined a better world.

If you liked this book, there are **two quick things** you can do to help me make more like it:

- Subscribe for FCP news and giveaways (click on the link, or just search for Forest City Pulp). We'll let you know when there are sequels, other new stuff, or FCP books are on sale. No spam or bullshit.
- Leave an honest review wherever you got this. Even if it's just one sentence, it *really* warms my heart and helps other people find the book.

Forest City Pulp publishes provocative fiction by provocative writers. It was founded in 2012 to take full advantage of the digital reality of publishing, and is designed to evolve as quickly as technology does. Visit www.ForestCityPulp.com or @ForestCityPulp for more information, and send us an electronic communication if you would like to get involved.

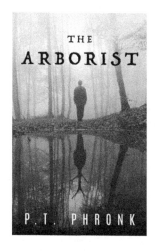

The tree was not there last night. Now, the terror is growing.

The Arborist is the standalone prequel to Three Incidents at Foster Manor. Discover what happened to Amy's family, and explore the origin of the terrifying mysteries that are gradually driving the world mad.

Get *The Arborist* here: https://forestcitypulp.com/books/the-arborist-by-p-t-phronk/

ABOUT P.T. PHRONK

P.T. Phronk writes about things that don't exist, things that might exist, and things that shouldn't exist. In other words, he writes fantasy, science fiction, and horror. Sometimes all three at the same time.

He received a PhD in psychology after writing a dissertation about why people like frightening films. So he literally wrote the book on horror, and continues to tinker with dark creations by cover of night, while by day, he writes about the mysteries of the human psyche as a brain scientist.

Get in touch with him any time on Twitter: @phronk

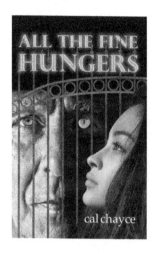

An old man—a monster—with power and privilege beyond imagination, preys on the weak, the innocent, the oppressed. One insatiable desire compels him above all others, and he'll stop at nothing to achieve it.

A timid girl who fears everything—having struggled since the day she was born against poverty, racism, colonialism, and misogyny—must decide to continue living in fear, or fight for what she deserves.

Each owes the state of their existence to factors compounded by the generations—factors that have left them at extreme opposite ends of the social divide. When they cross paths, only one will survive.

Get *All the Fine Hungers* by cal chayce here: https://forestcitypulp.com/books/all-the-fine-hungers-by-cal-chayce/

THANKS

Thank you to:

- Wording, for editing in such a way that it not only improved this book, but will improve all my writing from now on. You can permanently upgrade your own brain at http://www.wording.ca.
- Alexa, for proofreading. If you enjoy typos, then make sure you avoid her website at http://alexabooks.wixsite.com/authors.
- Everyone who read The Arborist and said something about it, whether it was a comprehensive review, or just asking "when's the next one?"
- Meg, for everything.

Made in the USA
Las Vegas, NV
22 January 2022